IN MY PROJECTS

Love and War in Harriston Homes

JAE TENE

In My Projects

Rizzo Johnson

Four Years Earlier

I sat here with my arms folded, legs forced closed, and the meanest mug on my face. Today was supposed to be one of the most joyous days in my life, but instead, I wore a scowl, and my mother was cursing me from here to hell. It didn't make me budge, and the doctors weren't coming in here. I was in active labor with my baby girl, but I was waiting for the love of my life to walk through the door.

"Rizzo, on everything I love, if you don't let them check on my grandbaby, I will tear this room up with you!"

My mother's dry threat didn't mean a thing to me. All my life she would talk her shit, but never laid a hand on me. I wasn't a bad kid, nor did I ever give her a hard time, so I was confused on why nobody was moving for my simple request. On top of everything else rushing through my mind like a vortex, I couldn't help but wonder where my besties were. If they knew like I knew, they would get here with what I asked for as well.

"Momma, can you at least call Tamiko? Lola's probably the reason they are being held up. I just want to make sure Croy knows that Tamia is on her way," I asked of my mother with pleading eyes.

My mother Rose was going on forty-eight but looked like she could be one of my girls. Her chocolate and toned skin was lighting up the dark labor and delivery room. I saw why my daddy worshiped the ground she walked on. Any other time I would be winning this eyeing game with her, but momma was not falling for it.

I never knew my biological mother, and as many times as momma and daddy tried, I pushed her away from exposing me to her life. The dumb ass bitch never wanted me to make it, and the day that Rose found me sitting in my pissy car seat crying my lungs out, that was all the information that I needed to know the bitch wasn't shit. I didn't care bout drugs or anything else that everyone tried to give for the excuse of a mother I had. Rose and Farrow, my father, were all I ever needed, and I didn't lack in anything I couldn't take with me when I left this earth.

"Stop giving her a hard time, Rizzo. Gone and let them check on her so you can relax. This is the shit I be talking about. Over here risking my granddaughter to make sure her 'ain't shit ass' daddy is here," my father went off, pissing me off even more.

You damn well I was waiting for Croy. He had let me down in every other aspect but promised for the first time that he wouldn't miss the birth of our daughter.

Croy and my relationship was everything but that. I met Croy a year and a half ago at a house party with Tamiko and Lola. We hit it off, but no one ever saw me out with Croy, nor did I ever meet a member of his family. After a while, I got fed up, and before I could do anything to rid myself of Croy for good, I found out I was pregnant. Croy had hidden me long enough, and when I went to tell him about my pregnancy, his ugly Pokémon looking girl-friend, Tiffiah met me.

After beating her ass about her nigga, I went home alone and cried my eyes out. I could never tell anyone for a good few months until Lola pulled it out of me. Tiffiah used her whole pregnancy to come for me on social media, and at one point, I fed into her shit by posting back and forth, throwing shade, knowing she was watching my page. Once I got fed up with her mouth, I blocked her on every-thing. I was told she made fake pages to lurk, but fuck that bitch and her thick ass eyebrows.

"What the hell are they out there waiting on? Oh! My bad Momma Rose and Daddy Row, I didn't know y'all made the cut to be in the room to meanie here," Lola sassed, walking into my room.

I rolled my eyes because she and Tamiko had let the nurses and doctors in with their aggravating asses.

"Your friend's in here being stubborn, and I don't even have the energy to check you. I'm dealing with sore ass over here. She is waiting for Croy to get here and is going to fuck around and land herself in the operation room!" Momma Rose gave me a stern look, and I just crossed my arms and looked the other way.

My parents excused themselves, and I finally let them check me, and I was still sitting at seven centimeters. Once they were done, they all walked out except Tamiko and Lola, who both look like they were about to spill whatever they were holding in.

"Baby girl, you want juice from downstairs?" my daddy asked, and I shook my head.

I didn't want anything but Croy to prove them all wrong and be there for me for once. I know I was being childish, but I didn't give a fuck, I loved Croy, even when he wasn't shit, so the least he could do was pay me the same respect.

I should've been done with Croy once I found out about Tiffiah, but when he came over begging for forgiveness, I had to give in. I hadn't fucked anyone in months, and I craved all ten inches of Croy. The way he caressed my body and treated me as if I was a rare delectable turned me on. I couldn't let him go, and now I was sitting here about to have a cow because he was yet again shitting on me.

Once my family was out of the room, Lola and Tamiko rushed to my bedside, phones in hand.

"Okay, so Croy's not coming. Before you start going off, fuck him, and we got you both," Lola said, and Tamiko shook her head.

"Why you gotta be so fucking hype all the time? Rizzo's already in labor, so be gentle, bitch." Tamiko squished her face up, and I was waiting for the rest of the tea.

"What do you mean, you spoke to him?" I asked, confused as fuck.

Both my girls looked and sounded so for sure of him not coming. Tamiko handed me her phone, and it was a live video of Croy in the same hospital waiting for his son to be born. I was pissed. Each comment congratulating them pissed me off, and I handed Tamiko back her phone. I rolled over, and Tamiko rubbed my back while Lola grabbed me some tissue.

"I swear he will ever see my daughter. On Rose Johnson, he will ever see her." I cried my eyes out, and Lola checked me quick.

"Rizzo, stop with this 'woe is me' routine you have going on. When Croy decided to fuck with you both, it should have been a wrap, but you chose to stay. These fucking tears ain't helping shit, and you putting our niece in distress, and then your ass going to have to get cut. Now there is nothing wrong with that, but do you really want to have to endure that recovery time, Riz?" she asked, and I shook my head.

One thing about Lola, she wasn't for that weak crying a shit unless you had to. This was no crying matter until I saw my baby girl's face.

"I hate to agree with her loud ass, but she right sis. You were warned as fuck, but the heart wants what the heart wants. For now, just focus on bringing Tamia in the world safe and sound. We got you the rest of the way."

Tamiko and Lola smiled at me, and I knew they meant every word and would live by it. As much as I knew now that what they were speaking was the truth, I couldn't shake this feeling. The hurt settled in to stay, and all the replayed in my head was the smile Croy wore waiting for his son. I could see the love he carried for Tiffiah, but I had seen that same look for me once upon a time.

An intense amount of pressure hit, sending pain down my back into my ass. I couldn't help but raise from the pain, and both Tamika and Lola looked shook. Tamiko went to get the doctor, while Lola freaked out like she usually did. I didn't know what the hell she would do when she was in this predicament. Everything seemed to move so fast, and before I knew it, Tamia Johnson was born and took my entire heart over.

I couldn't think of anything else as I stood there holding my pretty girl. Tamia looked every bit of Croy, but she was so healthy and chunky. Everyone loved on her and gave their little pet names out for her. I couldn't help but smile and bask in the moment. Momma came and sat next to me and smoothed my hair out while she told me how proud she was of me. I never saw myself doing this, but I felt so strong after giving birth as if I could do anything.

I snapped pictures and took me a nap. When I woke up, I had to hurry and grab the phone and snap the view before me. My father was laid out on my mother's lap with Tamia bundled up on his chest, and they were all knocked out.

Soon as I caught the picture, a nurse came in and asked me to wake them due to tests they needed to run on Tamia and visiting hours being over. I was sad to see them go, but it excited me to try to feed Tamia again. Breast-feeding was killing me, but I felt like I was getting the hang of latching her on for myself. Right now, the lactation specialist, Brenda, was doing the damn thing, and this little old white lady was everything and then some. I was trying to take her home with us, but I didn't think the hood was something she could get used to.

Once they left, Brenda walked in and asked if I wanted to change and feed Tamia before they took her for her hearing and vision check. I agreed, and we commenced to latching Tamia on after changing her. At first, Tamia struggled to find my nipple, but she soon latched on, and I felt like a superwoman again.

"Now just let her stay on there if she likes, but you still need to try to burp her every few minutes. She is a little pro. How are you feeling?" Brenda sat beside me, writing down Tamia's poopy and wet diapers.

"I feel okay now that I've had a nap. I do feel a little pain though, and my left nipple is a little raw. Is there anything I can put on them that safe for her?" I asked, and Brenda nodded, going into her cart for some packets.

"You can use this, but I always suggest letting the breast milk leak and rub it on. Breast milk heals more than people realize, and it's the safest thing for little miss molly here." Brenda smiled as she watched to make sure Tamia was still latched on.

Moving her a little, Brenda showed me what she meant, and the pain was there, but it cooled from the wet milk and air, giving me a little relief. Just as I finished feeding Tamia and Brenda had everything packed up, my room door opened and in walked Croy with a mean mug. I rolled my eyes, and Brenda gave a tight smile before telling me she would be on call if I needed anything. I nodded and placed my attention on the fuck nigga in front of me. With all the joy of Tamia's arrival, I had forgotten why I was upset before.

"Why you are pressing me, Rizzo?" this nigga let roll off his tongue, and as if Tamia knew it was her daddy, her eyes popped open, looking up at me.

"I wanted you to know that your daughter was born, but obviously you had better shit to do." I patted Tamia's back while she continued to look up at me.

Tamia was keeping me calm, and I was happy for that because all I wanted was to use this IV shaft to fuck his black ass up.

"It's funny how you go into labor the same day that Tiffiah is being induced. You wild yo, let me see if she's even mine," Croy boasted, walking up on Tamia and me.

When he got close enough, she wailed off crying at the top of her lungs, making Croy back up a little, and I laughed while trying to soothe her. I never saw Croy reach, but he grabbed me by the neck and squeezed.

"Laugh a little harder for me, Rizzo. You just don't get enough of trying to fuck up what peace I have. You need to go back to your place. You seemed to forget you come second around here," Croy said, and I was crushed, but this was nothing new.

Croy roughly let me go and walked away, pacing the

floor. Once he got far enough away, Tamia calmed down and placed her big brown eyes back on me. I wiped the tears away because her first memory will not be of me being weak. Fuck Croy and his stupid ass ways. I deserved better, and he deserved everything Tiffiah was about to bring his way.

"You know what, Croy, get the fuck out!" I yelled, hitting the call button.

Croy got too friendly with his hands, and I wasn't letting him knot me up with me baby girl right here. "All you want to do is tear me down and then be the one to build me up, only to knock me back down for your convenience. This is your daughter, and it will be up to you if you're going to be in her life. You only have six months to prove that though, outside of that, we fucking done, Croy! If it isn't about Tamia Marie, then I don't want anything to do with you."

My words were laced with pain, rage, and venom. I could literally see the poison sinking into Croy's bloodstream and everything clicking.

"Yo, I don't know who the fuck you think you checking, but I will—"

Croy was cut off mid-way to slap my ass, but the nurses walked in.

"Is everything okay, Ms. Johnson?" she asked, looking from me to him.

"No, I need him out right now!" I said as calmly as I could, and it was like she knew he was bad news because she already had security with her. They stormed in so fast and started to get Croy out, but dramatic ass Croy couldn't go without a bang.

"Man, I have a son coming any minute, y'all can't kick me out, yo! Rizzo, I swear on my son, I'm going to beat your ass bitch! Watch your step all summer, hoe!" Croy yelled leaving my room like the bitch nigga he was.

Croy would have beat my ass while I was holding my baby if the nurse hadn't come as fast as she did. I was done with Croy, and as I rocked Tamia to sleep, I made a promise to do everything that I could not to make her miss his ass. Fuck Croy!

2

Rizzo Johnson

Present Time

"Come on, mommy. *Baby shark do do do do dooo!*" Tamia jumped on my couch and sang at the top of her lungs while clapping her hands together like the dance goes.

I gave Tamia a look, and she pouted before hopping off my couch and to the floor where she finished her dance. I was busy making breakfast and cleaning her mess in the living room before Tamiko and Lola got here. It was typical from them to meet up here, or sometimes me at their house before we went into work. Since we all relied on Lola for a ride, we all worked the same shift unless something came up.

We all worked for Taco Bell/Pizza Hut, and I was sick and tired of it. I wanted more for myself and my girls, plus I was tired of hearing how great I was from customers and not getting anything from my job. At this point, it was just easy money and fast money.

I lived in Harriston Homes, and they are income-based. I have been here since I was five when my dad got locked up. When he got out four years ago, he was pissed because we were supposed to be taken care of and weren't.

After I had Tamia, I was granted an apartment, and I moved right in. Despite a few roaches every now and then, I loved my little apartment. Momma didn't like the environment and never did. I understood now that Tamia was older because my baby didn't know what it felt like to go outside and play freely. If they weren't shooting, fighting, or selling dope, the police were running up on folk and in houses, and they gave no fucks of who was in their way.

My daddy moved him and momma out to the country and had a nice layout, but I wanted my own, on my own, so I took what I could get. I also had Tamiko down the walk from me, and Lola across the street from me in Smith Homes. As bad as it was here, it was just as bad there, and sometimes they beefed. I didn't fuck with a bunch of bitches, I stayed lowkey, and everyone hated that but my girls. Tamiko's mother, Kenya, always said I was going to grow sick when Tamiko and Lola move away. They are not going anywhere without my ass.

My parents wanted me closer so that they could keep me safe, but I didn't have any worries. Croy had gotten on his shit two years ago. When he caught Tiffiah sucking off his best friend, it was enough for him to walk away. To think the nigga put a ring on it and everything, but I wasn't stupid. The bitch got pregnant again, claiming it's Croy's, and his dumb ass fell for the shit. It had Croy sniffing my way, but I been done with Croy.

Once upon I time, I gave a dead ass fuckship my everything, only to be hurt in every way in return. Croy broke me down, and all I wanted to do was give him a better life. I remember how many nights he snuck into our apartment down the walk and told me he was afraid of how his family would react to my skin tone. I was damn near white, but I had black in me some damn where. Shit like that would fuck with my head, but I wouldn't be giving him that key again. I fucked up one time with Croy and got pregnant again, but I aborted that shit. I wasn't dealing with this man for any longer than the first eighteen years I signed up for. Tamia was only two, so I wasn't ready for another kid, I wasn't Hoeffiah.

What was even crazier was the fact that this bitch was stalking Croy and me, which only confirmed the shit. One day he came over to my place stressed, saying how Tiffiah was mad that he got Tamia that weekend and didn't come and get Armon, their son. I shook that shit off because that bitch was pressed to have my life. I dye my hair, and here she goes, trying the same color. This bitch had a full list of my Fashion Nova wish list. Lola and Tamiko were both ready to beat her ass because she posted pictures of Tamia trying to clown my baby, but the bitch wouldn't step foot in my city.

I felt for the coo-coo bitch once before, since I found out she induced herself to have a one up on me. Tiffiah wanted her son to be born first so bad, so she downed some castor oil, and Armon ended up coming two weeks later but had ingested his own stool, so he was placed in the NICU and has had lifelong issues due to it. The night they found out about Armon's condition, I had Croy between my legs, and I knew then I had fucked up. I felt dirty and wrong, but the same week she went off about my baby, so it has been fuck that bitch ever since.

Croy tried me once again after that encounter, but I shut him down when I told him I just got rid of his baby. Croy was so hurt, but never really gave up on the idea of us and kept trying his hand when he came to get Tamia for his family time.

Today was one of his days, and I was dreading having

to try to curve his ass. Each time it was something new, and I was running out of ways to dodge his ass. There was a knock at the door as soon as I finished cleaning up, followed by Tamiko and Lola walking in.

"Hey, Stink!" Lola beamed, rushing over and lifting a cheesing Tamia into the air as if she weighed nothing. My baby had slimed up on us. She was all legs now.

"Auntie, I am too big for all of that. Wait, did you get my doll?" Tamia asked, raising one eyebrow like her father would when he was asking about something. I shook my head because, for a three-year-old, Tamia was a little woman.

"Girl, I have your ugly little doll and the crying one too. That thing kept me up all night, so it has to stay here with you," Lola countered, placing Tamia to the ground to grab her new toys.

"You probably weren't holding her right," Tamia said under her breath, and Tamiko and I fell out laughing.

"Bye Tamia, before I forget how cute your little ass is, and if I hear it cry one time, I am calling Child Protective Services!" Lola yelled to Tamia's back because she was already trying to haul the two dolls upstairs alone.

Lola went to help her while Tamiko came into the kitchen to make a plate. It was simple since we were going to work after Croy came to get Tamia. I made grits, bacon, cheese eggs, and French toast from the box. I was lazy as hell these past few weeks, but it was food. Lola came back and started rolling while Tamiko gave her the side-eye.

"What, damn?" Lola asked, looking dead at Tamiko.

"You about to roll again, right now, while I'm making plates?" Tamiko asked, and Lola looked lost.

"Uh, you are smoking or not? I can wait for my plate. Croy's always late, so we will be late. Just make mine last, this won't take me long." Lola waved Tamiko off.

"Now, this bitch going to want to wait too," Tamiko said, speaking on my life like she knew me, but the puppy dog eyes I gave her confirmed it. Tamiko placed her plate into the microwave and came to join the session.

"Y'all get on my nerves, little potheads." Tamiko laughed, shaking her head.

"Girl, you in on the blunt too now, how you are talking?" I asked, shaking my head.

There was another knock at my door, but this time the person waited. I figured it was my neighbor's grandmother asking for a cigarette, and I grabbed one to be ready to give her. Grandma always came at the same time, so I had her things waiting already.

My neighbor did my hair and had her grandmother living in the flats down the walk. She was the hood's grandma, and everyone knew it, so everyone looked out. Opening the door, I was faced with Croy smiling, showing off his new blue diamond fangs. I rolled my eyes and decided to fuck with his mental.

"You know the fangs are for bitches, right?" I asked, turning and walking away. I could feel Croy's eyes traveling my frame, so I turned to wiggle my finger.

"Man, ain't nobody sweating your white ass, yo. Where's my baby at?" he asked and then called her name.

Tamia said she needed to finish her overnight bag, which meant she was putting her baby and dolls in her little Moana suitcase. Croy made good money in the streets and spoiled Tamia and myself rotten, but I had cut back on taking from Croy. The fourteen hundred every two weeks was more than enough, and it was being saved as we spoke, so Tamia's college was paid for.

"Hey, have you thought about what she is doing for her birthday?" Croy asked, but Tamia's birthday was almost five months away. I wasn't planning shit that far out because my daughter was just as indecisive as her father.

"No, why, what's up?" I asked, confused as fuck.

"Tiff wants to have Armon's party the week of Tamia's birthday, and I want to make sure I make it for both," he said, and I rolled my eyes.

This was that weak, bitter shit I was talking about. If she thought this was going to get under my skin, she was wrong. I was used to this shit here.

"Do what you do, Croy. I need to get ready for work." I waved him off, trying to get back to the blunt I could smell before Lola and Tamiko smoked it all up. I needed at least that mellow high so that I could make it through my shift.

"Why you acting like that, Rizzo? I swear on my babies I don't want no issues, a nigga just trying to fuck work this all out," he said, and I laughed.

"See, there you go. Here I am trying to talk to you and you over here having a fucking comedy jam by yourself. You funny Rizzo, real fucking funny," Croy said in his feelings.

I hurried to use this time to check his slinky ass about himself. Croy was nothing close to big, but he held his own. His dark skin, and the way he kept his hair in the rough yet neat state used to turn me on. Now, the shit annoyed the hell out of me.

"Croy, you are my child's father, not my nigga! Shit, you never were, so this trying to talk our outside issues out is dead. If you want to work something out, just tell me the plan, and I will see how I can work with it. I told your ass, we don't have to do this shit while you're still in your feelings. You can do this with your WIFE!"

Croy walked up on me and wrapped his arms around my waist, placing his face inches from mine, and I turned my face. Croy smelled so good, and the feeling of his hands on the nape of my back was turning me on too much for comfort.

"You are playing with me, Rizzo, you know that pussy calling my name right now." Croy eased his hand into my basketball shorts and found my pearl and all the juices I had leaking. A small moan escaped my lips, and I grind against Croy's fingers.

"See, she misses daddy and you the reason she is being neglected. Pussy this wet means it's crying for some love and attention. You need me, Rizzo," Croy groaned in my ear, and I could feel his dick poking me over and over.

Croy bit down on my neck, increasing his speed, and my hips went in sync with Croy. I was mad at myself but too lost in the sensations to stop Croy. I needed this release, and the toys just weren't it for me.

"You need to let me drop this dick in you and make you forget all the other bullshit. You know I love you, Rizzo, and I want you in my life. I want yo to meet my family so they can meet Tamia." Croy said, and just like that, I was turned off. I no longer wanted that nut. I needed to make sure I heard this nigga correctly.

"Excuse me? So, where the fuck does you take her when you come and get her?" I asked, yanking his fingers from my body and pushing him. I was pissed. It was one thing when he hid me, but hiding my baby, our blessing, was a no go.

"I'm ready, daddy. Let's go!" Tamia rushed her legs away as she pulled at Croy so that they could go. It was just Croy's luck that they got away.

I fixed my hair and felt so fucking dirty and upset. I know like hell he didn't say meet his family. That shit was haunting my thoughts as I walked back into the kitchen to Lola smirking, and Tamiko shaking her head.

"What?" I asked, and Lola spoke up first as usual.

"You let him taste the pussy, didn't you?" She nodded with this creepy smile on her face.

"No nosey, worry about yourself. Croy and my ship had sailed and crashed to burn. There is no rescue, nor is there any coming back from it," I said more so to convince myself than them. I kept slipping up with Croy, but I never fucked him. After the abortion, I would let him taste the pussy every now and then, but that was it. I just needed to dead it completely so that these feelings would shut the fuck up and leave.

"Yeah, I hear you. Well, let's hurry up and smoke. Croy finally came on time, and I want to get in on time for once," Lola said, sparking the blunt as we talked and then got ready for our day at work.

I *needed to shake this nigga off me. They were noticing too much,* I thought to myself as I stayed in tune with the surrounding conversation until we finally left out for work.

3

Croy Moore

Rizzo was playing with me, but I wasn't giving up on her. Once I lost Rizzo, it was clear who was solid on my team, and it was not Tiffiah's money-hungry ass. When I found out she lied about the baby she carried after Armon, I had to chill on her. Rizzo knew that and joked about it all the time, but I hated that shit. Tiffiah was hounding me about coming home, but fuck all that shit.

I had left when Tiffiah tried to fight me and then put my daughter out of the house I had built and paid for. Man, it took everything in me to not beat the fuck out of Tiffiah when I walked to the door and heard Tamia on the other side crying her little heart out. I took my baby girl to her grandmother and went to get Rizzo. After she dragged Tiffiah, I packed my shit and left. I don't give a fuck how you treat me and what you do to my things but respect my children. This bitch stays on some sins of the father type bullshit.

Since then, she's been on my shit, but I've been lying low and chilling with a few baddies since Rizzo was not trying to give me any play. Ever since she killed my seed, and I blanked on her ass, Rizzo won't even let me taste her. I could finger fuck her and shit, but who does that?

I pulled up at my crib, and the shit looked rough. Grass was all out of hand, flowers were damn near dead now, and toys were laid out everywhere in the messy ass grass. I grabbed Tamia in my arms since she was asleep and went inside to get Armon.

I covered my nose before I could even close the front door because it smelled like old lettuce and spoiled milk. I had planned to lay Tamia down on the twenty-five hundred dollars couch I just had sent over, but it was covered in clothes, shoes, bags, and paperwork. I fixed Tamia's position and walked upstairs to find Tiffiah. I walked to Armon's room, and the only clear spot was his bed, but the sheet was missing. I went to lay Tamia down still so I could dig in Tiffiah ass, but I saw bugs moving on there and jumped back quick as hell grabbing Armon with me. Fuck it. Tiffiah could call me and find her son. The bitch had bed bugs, and I needed to get my kids and me clean now.

I hurried to my car with both the kids after shaking their clothes off and mine. I stopped and got them both a few outfits before going back to the small crib I was using for now. It was four bedrooms and larger than most, but small for what I was used to.

No sooner that I got inside and finally got them both bathed and changed, they were asleep. My phone started to blast Tiffiah's ringtone, and I hurried to answer so I could dig in her ass.

"Bitch, you have some nerve dialing my fucking number! Where the fuck you at?" I asked, and I heard her blow out air as if she didn't give a fuck.

"Croy, I was just next door getting some sugar to make Kool-Aid. You could have taken Nadia with you, she is your step-daughter. She was in here screaming and alone," Tiffiah's dizzy ass really said, and I walked to my room to sit down.

"Tiffiah, you need to stay with them. Call your neighbor, or smoke signal their ass, I don't give a fuck. You need to stay with them damn kids. Why is the house so fucking nasty though? If you can't handle the maintenance, then say something, and you can get something smaller. My step-daughter, but you haven't been a wife nor step-mother in years."

"Croy, you don't have a stay in this house or do the upkeep of it. I have been busy, but I am getting to it as we speak. Please have my son back home tonight. I don't know what the other child's momma has in her house." Tiffiah hung up, and I looked at my phone as if she was still there and could see me.

When I first met Tiffiah, I was cut off from my family's money for acting reckless with it and using her ass to make sure that I was able to eat and sleep comfortably. Tiffiah was fighting bitches for me and had even stuck it through with all my cheating. When I stepped up in my family due to my father being sick, it was only right I brought her with me. The only thing is, when I got money, Tiffiah became lazy. I had to get a maid, and Tiffiah quit her job at UPS because she didn't need the money from the bands I brought in.

Once I started fucking with Rizzo, I saw Tiffiah less, and the only reason I went back to Tiffiah was because my family pushed me, and she told me she was carrying my son. I was happy as fuck, but I didn't expect Rizzo to pop up with the same news, the same night. Rizzo whooped Tiffiah's ass so bad that I had to take her ass to the hospital to make sure my son was straight. To this day, Tiffiah swears Rizzo was at fault that Armon tried to come the same week as Tamia, but I found out the bitch drunk castor oil.

There was a knock at the door, and I saw my brother Orion and his best friend Truth standing on my porch.

Orion was a good brother to most people that knew us, but to me, he was a show-off. Orion thought he was too good to be in the hood and ran his part of the operation from home. The nigga didn't put in a once of legwork, him or his tight eyes best friend Truth. Truth was Lola's brother, and I didn't like his quiet ass. The nigga never spoke but would hit your ass with the quickness. Orion fucked with him for that fact alone, but I didn't. It was crazy because as much work as I put in for my family and our name, Orion was the one that got the praise. Shit, Truth was getting more hype, and that nigga sat beside Orion the majority of the time. I could have sworn them niggas was fucking on each other.

I answered the door and let them in, dapping them both up.

"What brings you ugly niggas by?" I asked, sitting down while they both did the same. Truth sat on the arm of my couch, and that nigga knows I hate that.

"I heard you had my nephew and niece, and you know I hate when that bitch calls my phone," Orion said, shaking his head and pulling out his phone. Truth nudged him, and I mugged his ass.

"Oh, we need you to move off of Terrell Street for a little while," Orion said like it wasn't shit. Orion knew damn well that Terrell Street and the surrounding area was where I made the most of money. Cutting off my supply there would fuck up my revenue.

"Fuck you mean, I ain't shutting down shit. Terrell Street is where I make the most of my money, and if you cut that shit off, then you can't expect the same load. Why the fuck am I shutting down shop, fuck going on that I don't know about?" I asked, looking between the two. Truth was in his phone, while Orion sealed and lit the blunt.

"Shit is hot for right now. I heard we have some niggas watching where you camp and that shit needs to get handled first. Until then, just work on the east and make sure English Street is nothing but our men and stocked. Ray and Jay are loading your shit up as we speak."

Orion passed me the blunt, and I pulled choking instantly. Shit, Orion fucking with them Haitian cats again, their weed is killing folk out here.

"The fuck these niggas mad about? Either way it goes, I ain't shutting shit down. I have some shit lined up, and I need to make sure that goes through. After that, I got you. I will get more niggas to look out and chill, but outside of that, I need that bag."

Orion and Truth stared daggers into my body as if I was speaking with disrespect.

"You going to have to deal with JB about that, little brother. I got you no matter what, but be smart about this. Look, I'm about to go and check on your little badass twins." Orion jumped up, leaving Truth's silent ass right here with me while I toked the blunt.

This shit they were bringing to me was some bullshit, and I was down for whatever when it came to JB. JB was like an uncle to us all, but he ran the operation here and would be passing it on soon. I planned to be the son to inherit just that. I had earned it.

Orion was smart, but so was I. The streets ran smoothly because of my brain, my ideas, and my commands. If Orion or Truth had to deal with these niggas, they would be dead on the first night. Those niggas weren't hood built.

Truth chuckled, and I jumped, making him look back and smirk. I had never heard this nigga make a sound, and the shit was wild and creepy. I didn't fuck with him. I just let him do him. Orion came downstairs, and I heard the kids yelling and talking shit back to him. I laughed because Armon would throw the jokes, and Tamia was just agreeing.

"Hey, we are hitting this club tonight. Are you trying to slide with us?" Orion asked, swinging Tamia around while Armon wrapped his body around his leg.

"Nah, I gotta take them to see ma and shit. Duck it up for me though, niggas."

Orion nodded, and they finally stopped playing. He sent the kids back to their room, and they made their way out. We made plans to meet at the warehouse tomorrow morning to get my shipment from them. I hated to have to do shit. It made me feel like the field nigga while Orion and Truth were the house niggas.

Rizzo came to my mind, and I thought about how she used to tell me that maybe my family saw me as their protector and therefore placed me in the field to protect them. I swear Rizzo could see the positive in anything negative I bring her way. I missed her sexy ass, and days like this, I wish I had picked her instead of Tiffiah that day. If I had, I know I would still be with Rizzo, and we would be a happy family. Rizzo would never have had to abort my seed, and I would have never told her she was my best-kept secret, ruining any future I wanted with her.

Sometimes I feel like I still have a hold on Rizzo. Each time I tickle her pearl, and she moans over my lips, for just that moment, I feel as if I have her all to myself. I think it was time I stepped up and made it right with Rizzo. I had the best moments of my life when I was sneaking with her, so to finally be able to get her the lifestyle she deserved might make her love me again. I know her bright ass was tired of living in Harriston Homes. That shit was hood as fuck, and I hated when niggas asked about my shorty in the slums.

I turned a movie on for the kids and me until it was time to go and see my parents.

4

Tiffiah Moore

"That nigga pressed, ain't he?" I laughed to my best friend, Charnell, and she joined in shaking her head.

Croy had really come in here worried about my house. I knew I had let it get out of hand, but I had a lot of shit going on. This nigga I was fucking with found out I took some money from him, and it was no petty cash. This nigga Mack was big, black, and ugly and had niggas looking for me as we speak. I was lowkey happy Croy took Armon. I didn't want my baby to get hurt behind my dumb ass.

"So, fuck him, and what is the plan, bitch? That nigga knows where I work and everything, so we need to figure out what we're going to do?" Charnell voiced, looking scared as hell. I didn't have one fucking clue, and at this point, I was thoughtless.

"Bitch, I have no clue. That money is gone, and if he comes for us, we have nowhere to fucking hide. My momma still looking for me for her money and shit for keeping Armon for six months last year." I paced the floor, trying to think of something.

"You don't think that Croy would give you the money, or I don't know, tell that nigga Mack that Croy set him up. You want that nigga out your life anyway. Make Mack think Croy took Armon and made you do it," Charnell said, and I thought about that shit.

I knew Mack's big ugly dog looking ass was in love with me, so I was going to use that shit. Croy had me fucked up if he thought he was playing me. I was hip to his fucking game.

See, when I wasn't giving Croy what he wanted, and I didn't raise Armon the way he wanted me to, he would leave and hit up that horse looking ass Rizzo bitch. Croy had been fucking with this bitch for a while, and after she laid hands on me, I should have pressed charges. Instead, Croy moved me two cities away to make sure we didn't run into each other. The thing about it was, I was in her town often, and I watched how she lived. The bitch should be ashamed.

Rizzo lived in income-based apartments that were known for being nasty and filled with bugs. This was my second bed bug issued, and that's only because my neighbor has them. I could never sleep with roaches though. Tamiko and Lola aren't any better, and they think they hot shit. Both stay in the same hood or across the street in the Smiths, and I wouldn't know which is worse.

Truth's sexy ass was Lola's brother, so why didn't he get her out the hood and have her laid up somewhere lavish like Croy was living? I guess when you're not in the streets as heavy as my husband, then you weren't bringing home as much.

I pulled my phone out and posted how cute Tamia was when Croy came to get Armon on my Facebook page and made sure I made the post public. I knew Rizzo's flock of followers were watching me waiting for me to say something about their queen. Rizzo's support system pissed me off. I mean, people were always liking her shit and sharing her boring ass post. They even applauded the hoe when she threw shade right back at me. Petty is petty. You can't have variations.

A loud bang came from the living room, making me and Charnell look and jump out of our skins. You could hear niggas flooding my house and coming upstairs where we were. Once they got to my room, they drew their guns on me, and I counted at least eight niggas with their weapons on us.

"Please don't kill us! Please don't shoot!" Charnell's ass cried, and I shook my head.

"Bitch, get the fuck up!" I yelled, but she kept crying and shit.

I was scared as fuck too, but I knew these niggas and the reason they were here. Mack wanted his money, and if I am dead, he doesn't get that. We needed to be smart, and this bitch was folding up on me. I knew I shouldn't have let her come along with my ass.

Charnell was a big bitch, but she could dress her ass off and wore nothing but wigs. I think she could tone the makeup down, but that was her. At this point, our friendship was on robbing niggas, but this bitch was about to get cut. I was two seconds from telling them to kill this bitch when Mack made his grand entrance. Fear had finally set in with me when I saw him in the flesh. Maybe I wasn't walking out of here today.

"You look like you worried, Tiffiah. How you been, shorty? Come here, give me some love, yo." Mack opened his arms, and it confused me. This nigga didn't look like he was pissed or anything. He's gotta be high.

"Mack, why are they in my house with their guns on

my best friend and me?" I asked, hoping he would fall for my shit.

Mack laughed and scratched his chin while looking through me.

"Nah, you run fast shorty, and a nigga done put on a few pounds, so I can't keep up. But check this, I heard you misplaced something of mine, and I was wondering if I could get that back and be on my way," he said and sat on my bed. I just knew my shit would fall off the beams, but thankfully, they were intact.

"I don't know what you're talking about, and unless you here to apologize for that bitch, then get the fuck on, Mack. I mean that shit! I am just healing from the shit you put me through. I can't see you right now," I faked and made my tears fall as I turned from him.

Mack had a little piece on the side in New York that he thought I didn't know about. I knew, but I needed to act like I didn't.

"Bitch, you trying me right now. I never fucked around on you. I loved you more than I ever loved anyone, and you stole from me?" Mack's voice elevated, and I turned to look at him with the most hurt look I could muster.

"So, you weren't going to see Alicia when you went to New York? By the way, congrats on the kid. Maybe that's why you are just coming to see about the girl that got away," I said, and Mack's whole face changed. Mack dropped his head and shook it at the same time, and I just looked up and wiped my face.

"D, y'all take shorty right here downstairs, close the door, and let me chop it up with shorty." The guy was hesitant but followed his orders. Once they were gone, and the door was shut, Mack pulled me into his big chest and held me while I cried.

"You said you loved me and would never hurt me. You

never hit me, and you never made me do anything I didn't want to do. I fucked you, fed you, and listened to you, but still, that wasn't enough for you to be happy, and know that I was. Marquise, you really fucked up my mental, and the only thing I knew would hurt you was to take your money. The one thing you loved the most, more than me, and probably more than Alicia's ass."

"Tiffiah, I fucked up, and I planned to come home and tell you, but you were gone. I thought you just ran off with my money and got good with your lick. Fuck, I never knew you had any idea about her." Mack said, feeding into my lies, and I held back my sinister smile. Mack was making this easier than I thought it would be. Now I just had to lay on the icing.

"Mack, why did you have to come back? Why couldn't you just leave me alone? I can't take this." I cried harder, and Mack held me tighter, almost suffocating my ass.

After that, Mack and I talked, and he decided to let Charnell and I live. Alicia was living with him, but things weren't working out, so he asked me to give him some time, and he wanted me and the kids to come to live with him. I only agreed so that I could make it out of here alive. After fucking Mack silly, he and his men left, and Charnell was right back in my room asking questions while I smoked a cigarette.

"So, he's just over the shit if you move to New York with him?" Charnell asked, pacing the floor again.

"Basically, but I ain't doing that shit. I will just ask Croy for the money to move and tell him I think Armon should stay with his ass. After I get the money from him, I'm gone, and you should try to do the same," I said, looking Charnell up and down. She shook her head and sat at the foot of my bed, taking her phone out.

"Bitch, I know Croy doesn't have Rizzo watching your son?"

I jumped up naked as the day my mother birthed me to snatch Charnell phone from her grasp. I looked at the live video, and sure enough, Rizzo was holding Armon while Lola held Tamia, and Tamiko recorded them having a grand time at the fair. I was livid because Croy knew not to take my son around that hoe, nonetheless, leave him with her.

"Oh, I'm on her ass."

I jumped up, grabbed a maxi dress, and threw it over my body. Since I was a hairstylist, I had done some quick box braids in my hair, so I threw them up into a bun and grabbed my keys. Before heading downstairs, I looked back at Charnell as she sat still watching the video.

"Bitch, bring your ass. If you are not coming with me to beat this bitch ass, then take your ass on home," I said, and she laughed at me.

"I'll go, but only because I don't want her to drag your ass in public."

I rolled my eyes as Charnell squeezed past me. I didn't know why she was trying to play me. I had fought Rizzo before, and while she had some hands on her, I had something new for her ass.

━━

I GOT to the carnival in an hour, and I was searching high and low for this high yellow hoe and her stable of friends. Charnell was pulling her hair up, but I hoped she was ready for whatever because I damn sure was. When I spotted them, they were taking pictures of the kids on the kiddy ride, and I took full advantage of tagging Charnell along.

Walking up on all three with their backs turn, I went into my purse and opened my blade. I slashed Rizzo's shoulder and then Lola's arm before Tamiko turned and struck me as fuck in the jaw. Charnell hit her, but Tamiko was ready and whooping her ass. I felt my hair being dragged, but when I looked up, I saw Rizzo lift her leg and kick the shit out of my stomach.

"Let the bitch up, Lola!" Rizzo shouted, and when she did, I jumped up and rushed Rizzo, smiling at the blood leaking from her shoulder.

Rizzo dodged me, turned so quick, and then started to rain blows on me. I waved my hands to try to stop her, but that was no use. The sound of my son and Tamia crying must have stopped her because after I heard them, the hits stopped. Charnell came and helped me up as Armon ran over to me with tears in his eyes.

"Stay the fuck away from my son, uppity bright bitch!" I yelled.

"Shut the fuck up, Tiffiah. She just whooped your ass, and you still popping shit. I should come finish your hoe ass off about my fucking arm. If you can't beat me, then you shouldn't have brought your stank ass over this way. You know what—"

Lola pushed past everyone holding us apart and ran up on me. I thought I would dodge her, but when I moved left, she did too and knocked me clean between my eyes and nose. I heard a crack before everything went black.

5

Rizzo

"Rizzo, you really got me fucked up if you expect me to calm the fuck down knowing that some bitch out here cutting you up. Where he fucks is Croy's bitch ass?" my father Farrow asked, and I shook my head as my mother cleaned up my cut.

Tiffiah weak ass ain't hitting on shit, and I guess she didn't slice skin often because she didn't do much damage. I couldn't believe she tried me today while I had Tamia with me. Each time I envisioned it, the more anger stewed in my stomach. I wanted to beat the fuck out of Tiffiah, but the sound of Tamia begging me to stop is what stalled me. I wouldn't ever have done that in front of her, and it saddened me that Tiffiah took me there.

"Daddy, bump Croy. If he knew about it, he would have stopped her, or at least told me," I said, and Lola and Tamiko both smacked their lips while my daddy looked at me like I had grown three heads.

"Baby girl, I know like hell you are not that dumb. Croy only gives a fuck about himself. Hence, you having both of his kids on his weekend. Croy's gotta see me, and you don't have a fucking say in what I do."

I rolled my eyes and watched him grab his coat and leave out the side door to the garage.

"Let him cool off. You know your father doesn't play about his baby girl. I really didn't think the child had it in her, to be honest. Tiffiah talks a big game online, she and that momma of hers," my mother said, and Lola and Tamiko laughed.

"Aye, auntie, when she said you were built like roll-on deodorant, I died!" Lola joked, and my momma threw a bandage roll at her.

"Meanwhile, that fat, unhealthy hoe is rolling around on a cart in Wal-Mart. I swear she's mad about Farrow choosing me back in the day. That nigga had us both wild at one point, but I stopped that. I left when she tried to claim pregnant with someone else's sonogram. The sick bitch must have passed on the genes," my mother said, and we all burst out laughing.

"I mean, I gave her Croy back, so what is the real beef?" I asked, laughing, but everyone else looked at me, smirking.

"You ain't give her shit back if he still trying to drain your soul. Rizzo, you are playing with that boy, and you know he is going to want more out of you. Croy treated you like shit, and if you for one second think about taking him back, then you agree to take back on all the pain too. I love you, but I would hate to have to sit back watching this happen to you," my mother said, and at the same time, Tamiko's mother, Kenya, walked in ready to find Tiffiah and her momma.

"Now momma, if you don't calm yourself down. You know that girl momma cannot fight a soul out here. What you are doing home from work early?" Tamiko asked, and Kenya raised a brow.

"Um, I birthed you, not the other way around. I came because my sister called me. Why the fuck them bitches get to cut Lola and Rizzo though?" she asked, and Tamiko rolled her eyes, making Kenya smack her arm. "Don't make me take them out your face, Tami!" Kenya fussed.

"Ma, chill, I handled mine and theirs. I wasn't letting no bitch take out my sisters." Tamiko did this strut that had us all laughing because it was DaBaby's "Suge" dance.

We all sat around and talked about it, and Tamia ran in and out trying to get more candy from my mother's living room table. I told her she didn't need to have this shit out in the open for Tamia to eat, but she swears it's her grand parental right. I didn't argue any further because she and my father loved that girl with every breath in their bodies.

"I can't get over the fact that she left her kids with her momma for six months chasing a nigga. That shit is weak as fuck," Lola said.

I agreed, I would never do anything like that, if my baby can't come, then I couldn't come either.

"I guess she figured things would work out for her. My question is, why did she come back?" Kenya asked, and we all shook our heads.

"Maybe it wasn't all it was cut out to be. Can we stop talking about that girl for one minute? Matter of fact, Rizzo you are cleaned and bandaged. I think you three need to give me and Kenya time with Tamia. Get out, hit the town tonight, and forget all about that girl and her drama. Every time something like this happens, you three sit in here and do just this. If you are not going to put a finish to her, then let her messy ass be mad. She isn't about that life anyway," my mother said, and I agreed with her.

I hated that I took things this far with Tiffiah, and from now on, I was done feeding into her bullshit. Next time, I was taking out my pearl and shooting the anteater in the fucking neck.

"Ma, you sure you have Tamia tonight, you had her all week?" I asked, and she nodded.

"I don't mind at all, baby. Just go and enjoy yourself and try to find me a son-in-law," my mother joked and kissed me on the forehead.

While Lola ad Tamiko waited for me, I went to Tamia's room and made sure she was okay.

"Hey mama, what are you doing?" I eased down to the floor beside her.

"On my tablet. You are leaving?" she asked, looking up at me and dropping her tablet. Tamia put her two warm hands on my face, and it made me smile as it always did.

"Yeah, Granny wants to hold you longer, unless you want to come home?" I offered, and Tamia shook her little head so fast.

Looking around her L.O.L. themed room and all her electronics and clothes and shoes. My baby loved coming to be with her paw and granny. I kissed her forehead and made sure she was good before leaving with the girls.

Just as I got into the car with Lola and Tamiko, my phone started to ring, and from the ringtone, I knew it was Croy's ass. Lola blew out an air of frustration, and Tamiko just went into her phone as always, trying to mind her business. I knew why he was calling, and I wasn't in the mood for his shit, so I ignored the call. That wasn't enough because Croy just started to blow me up some more.

"Girl, pick up before he has a damn asthma attack." Lola rolled her eyes, and I picked up.

"What Croy, and if you are calling to ask why I put your baby momma down, then hang the fuck up because I am with all the shits!" I yelled as Lola pulled up to the store near my mother's house.

I didn't go in because I was on the phone, but I should have.

"Man, shut that shit up and come here." I looked out the passenger window, and sure enough, Croy was parked right beside us, giving me the meanest mug he could.

I got out at the same time he got out. Croy had me fucked up if he thought he was running shit this way. He lost that privilege a long time ago, so for him to be coming at me sideways was a no-go for me.

"Croy, you have some fucking nerve to be—"

Before I could finish, Croy slapped me so fucking hard that I fell to the gravel ground scraping my left elbow. I held my face, and I could taste the blood seeping from my lip to my mouth. I looked back up at Croy just as Lola and Tamiko walked out.

"What the fuck? Croy have you lost your—"

Lola was running up on Croy when he pulled his .380 out and aimed it right at her ass.

"I know how you bitches get down, and I don't have time for it. Rizzo, get your ass up and in the fucking car. Play if you want to, and your momma will be healing a gunshot wound."

I was heated beyond measurement, and I knew it was all over my face. I got up, got myself together, and grabbed when I needed from Lola's car.

"You not about to leave with him, are you, Rizzo?" Tamiko grabbed my arm and asked.

"I don't want you two mixed up in my bullshit, and I can handle myself. I'll be home in a few. Meet me there," I tried to sound convincing, but Lola damn sure wasn't buying it, and Tamiko didn't look convinced either.

I gave them a reassuring look, and they nodded to let

me go. I walked over, and I made sure to keep a straight face. Croy knew I didn't go down without a fight, so I was waiting for my right moment.

When I got into the car, I watched Croy back away and put the gun down as he got inside himself and pulled out. Turning his radio all the way up, Croy watched the road while driving to his duck out spot. Croy kept a duck out place for when he wanted to spend more time with me. At first, it was cute, but when you learn you are his best-kept secret, it was something a horror story. I used to love coming here, it was my escape from everything at home, or so I thought. Now, the duck out spot was where we fought the most. Croy knew I could handle my own, and we went toe-to-toe when we needed to. Judge all you want, but I got my anger out, and Tamia wasn't exposed to it.

WE PULLED up a dreading thirty minutes later, and Croy hopped out, as did I. When Croy walked around the car trying to grab me, I yanked my arm back. There was nothing he needed to do to me while we were in plain sight. He could wait until we got inside like always. I hurried to the door to get inside. It was clear that Croy had an issue with the way we handed Tiffiah her own ass whooping. I wasn't about to play with this nigga anymore. After this, I was done, and I wanted him out of my life. Croy could take the blood thirsty tick he is married to with his ass.

When Croy unlocked the door, and we got inside, I wasted no time grabbing the vase and smashing that shit over Croy's head. Watching him stumble didn't stop me, I jumped on that nigga like flies on fresh shit!

"You really mistook me for that bitter ugly horse you

fucked and married, huh?" I scream, punching Croy all in his fucking head. I was trying my hardest to at least leave the nigga with a concussion.

Croy drew back and slapped me so fucking hard I spun around and fell over the table, which once held the vase that I crashed over his head. Karma was a bitch.

"Get the fuck up. You damn right, the way you out here acting in front of my kids, bitch you got me fucked up. I take a lot of your shit, but you need to grow the fuck up, Rizzo!"

I turned and wanted to charge Croy with everything in me, but for once, I just looked at this nigga.

"Croy, she attacked me while I was watching your kids enjoy their time at the carnival! You knew that bitch didn't want me near your son, why would you even leave him with me?" I asked, holding my face.

Croy laughed like I was a new comedy special or something.

"I do what the fuck I want with my kids, Rizzo. They're mine! I don't have to explain shit to you nor her!"

"Then why the fuck are we even here? Croy, why can't you just move the fuck around yo? You ain't shit and never will be shit, but you need to step the fuck up. I am done coming here with you when you get mad, having to explain the fucking bruises! My daddy wants your fucking head behind this shit, and my dumb ass was over there begging him to leave it be. Look at us, Croy! This shit is not us, and I'll be damned if I continue to accept your shit. I stayed your secret, but I don't owe you shit. You're married for fuck sake. We are done! Take me home now!"

I meant every word I had just spoken. I was done being this nigga punching bag one day and his fuck buddy the next. I hated I loved this nigga as much as I did, and the tears flowing down my face told him that.

Croy walked over to me as I broke down. I was tired of this shit, and deep in my heart felt we could work this shit out one day. It's like, Croy goes weeks on his shit, then boom, he is fucking up again. That shit grows old, and it isn't something I can get used to or subject Tamia to.

Croy placed his arms around me and lifted my head, looking me in my eyes. *Damn, this nigga is fine.*

"I could never quit you, Rizzo. You will always have a hold on me." Croy kissed me so passionately, and it was no fighting him.

The spearmint taste mixed with the weed, the feel of his hands roaming my body, and the way my body responded was driving me crazy. I knew this was a mistake, but I couldn't stop myself.

Croy lifted me, carried me to the bedroom, and laid me on the bed. Croy kissed me down to my pussy, and I arched my back. The way his tongue swirled on my pearl and him suddenly sucking the soul out of my shit made me scream in ecstasy. I could feel Croy insert two fingers into my wet pussy, and I grind myself into them as I felt myself about to cum. I looked down and rubbed Croy's head. The sight of his staring me down made me cum harder than I thought I would. Croy didn't miss a beat flipping me over and sliding deep into my pussy from behind.

"See, she can't go without this dick neither. Why are you trying to run from a nigga?" Croy asked, beating down my fucking walls.

Croy had an eight-inch monster that was thick as fuck. I was terrified to fuck him our first time, and I just knew he would split me open. Since it had been a while, the pain was still there.

"Slow down, shiiiiiit, slow doooowwn!" I moaned as Croy worked my pussy as only he knew how. The pain was coming down, and pleasure was setting in making me cum yet again.

"Damn baby, you were supposed to wait for a nigga. Throw that ass back, Rizzo," Croy grunted, and I did just that. Croy's dick was finding my spot with each stroke. Croy reached up and grabbed my hair, yanking it back.

"Fuuuuuck!" I screamed. Croy pushed my back down and started to go even harder.

"Shit, I'm about to cum, Rizzo!"

Croy let go of my hair and gripped my ass, keeping his speed. I knew this nigga didn't wrap up, and I was cursing myself out for the shit. Just as I was about to scream for him to pull out, I began to cum so hard my legs went limp, and I fell forward. Croy fell on top of me and came, while I rode out the orgasm of the year.

"Damn it!" I tried to get up, but I was sore, and my legs wouldn't work for the life of me. Croy laughed at my ass, but I was too weak to slap him for it.

"Ain't shit funny, nigga!"

"Yeah, your noodle leg having ass is hilarious! I'll get you a rag." Croy slapped me hard on the ass and went to use the bathroom and get a warm rag.

What surprised me was how Croy rolled me over and cleaned my pussy for me. This was not the man I was used to at all. Croy put the rag away and came to bed to lay down.

"You know I want you in my life Rizzo, but I made a promise, and I just need to find a way to get out of it. Please just work with me and don't give up on a nigga. I got you if you got me," Croy said, and I simply nodded and listened to him drift off to sleep.

Once Croy's snore grew loud as a bear, I slide from his arms and high tailed out of the duck out spot. I called an Uber to four houses down and went back to my house.

Lola and Tamiko weren't there, but that was fine with me. I couldn't face them after the nasty ass fucking session I had just had with the nigga I had no business being with.

I took my time for myself to go and shower properly. While inside, I thought about where I was and what I needed to do so that I could see some change in my life. Croy was toxic to me, and although he just fucked me better than he ever had, I was done dealing with the drama that came with it. If we were to ever make things work, I knew I would catch hell from my family, and Tiffiah wouldn't rest until we were done. I had to let Croy go, and as hard as it might be, I got this.

6

Lola Lee

"Truth, I am grown, and if I want a nigga in my spot, I can have one!" I stormed out of my bedroom to the kitchen to check on the food I was cooking.

Truth had been up my ass all fucking day about the bruises over my body, and I would have covered them up had I known he would be home. Truth was my big brother, and I loved him with every fiber in my body. My brother worked hard for his money, but he liked to live in the hood. He swears that was the best way to keep his ear to the streets, but I knew it was just in case our mother returned.

Our mother left about two years ago with some nigga and never turned back. Last we heard, she was on drugs and divorced. Our father's mother looks out for us, but she had Alzheimer 's disease and couldn't always be on top of things. We are staying in Smith Homes, but everyone around here called it the Smiths.

I remember when we first moved here, Truth and I got it bad because we were half-Asian. People thought we weren't with the shit, but we had to show the better than we spoke on it. Truth had always been quiet, so when they picked on him, and he got fed up and fucked them up, they knew not to fuck with him. I was tried based on the simple fact that I was bad as fuck with long, natural hair.

"See, it's 'Truth I'm grown' until one of these bitches snatch that fucking hair up, and you want someone to help you get back." Truth sat down on the couch and started to count out some money.

I knew my brother was deep in the game, but I didn't know any of his homies, except Croy's ugly ass, due to his big ass fucking mouth.

Croy was never on my good list, and it would take God himself to make that change. I hated watching Rizzo drool over his ass, and at one point, I was going to body the boy myself. Croy was dirty and smelled of evil, and I couldn't wait for my bitch to get it. Rizzo was an amazing mother and one of the best friends I had ever had. So, watching her struggle with that nigga pissed me off.

"Truth, get the fuck on with your shit, okay? I have to get to work, and you all in my way. Get up off my apron so I can go, damn!" I bent over and snatched my apron from under his ass. Truth was being an asshole, and I needed him to find somewhere to go, now!

"You want a ride so Rizzo can use the car?" he asked, and I looked at Truth like he grew two heads.

"Uh-uh, you know that bitch cannot drive."

I wasn't lying either. I loved Rizzo, but she drove like a bat out of hell, and she wasn't about to put another dent in my shit. Truth cursed me to the depths of hell and back when he saw it, so I didn't know why he was offering my shit up.

"Since you are feeling generous, let me drop you off and let her crash your shit," I threw back, and Truth closed his eyes and played sleep.

Yeah, just like I thought.

I walked out the door and called Rizzo so she could be walking out the door when I pulled up, I hated to be left to wait. The hood was already out, and it was nine in the morning. It wasn't scorching hot out, but the sun was already beaming down on my hood, and I prayed my baby didn't run hot once I hit this highway. That would make Truth the happiest man on earth because then he could get me into something newer.

When I pulled up, Rizzo was locking her door before stepping off her small, one-step porch. I saw her neighbor's daughter run up to her and hugged her, and I laughed as I watched Kayla twirl her long, pretty hair, and all the other kids run up to be around her.

Kayla was the most popular kid in Harriston Homes, and she was only five. It wasn't just her appearance, because Kayla was one of the cutest little girls out here, but she was sweet as pie literally. Kayla was so sweet that I worried about how life would treat her. I hoped she stayed as sweet as she was, but knew when to buckle up on these humans that roam this earth.

Rizzo finally came to the car, and I was seconds from blow my damn horn. I knew she saw me out here waiting, and even Kayla wasn't going to hold me up.

"Hey girl, where's Tamiko?" Rizzo asked with a busted lip. I rolled my eyes because I knew she didn't think I was going to bypass that.

"Bitch, what the fuck is up with your lip?" I turned all the way around to make sure she knew I wanted answers. Rizzo rolled her eyes like she wanted to lie, but if she fought Croy, I was getting in her and his ass.

"Nothing, I'm good. I fucked up though." Rizzo looked at me with puppy dog eyes, and I sped out the parking lot.

I turned my trap music up and ignored Rizzo's dumb ass while speeding down Randleman Road. Rizzo was pissing me off, and thankfully Tamiko and her Mother Teresa personality was not in attendance. I was getting in her ass soon as I hit Highway 29. The exit didn't come fast enough, and the attitude Rizzo carried was evident, but I don't give a fuck!

"Rizzo, you really are fucking dumb as fuck!" I yelled, turning my music down. Rizzo looked at me like I lost all sense, but that wasn't stopping me.

"Excuse me?" she asked, her voice laced with attitude. "Croy is my baby daddy, and if I decide to throw this pussy for him, that is my choice!" she fired back, and I let out a nice and hearty laugh.

"You funny as fuck with all that mouth, but I was holding you after you gave birth, and he went missing for Tiffiah and her fake labor! I have been there where he forgot to grab your child some pampers and milk and said you and Tamia would have to wait! I sat up with her when she first got sick because I knew my bitch was tired and needed some rest. I didn't do any of that shit to watch you run right back to the man that's giving his all to a piece of a shit mother! You know that same dick is being thrown to that bitch, and you still hopping on it! What example are you setting for Tamia, huh? Yeah, that shit didn't register while he was digging in them guts, huh. You fucked up? Tuh, you did more than fuck up if you didn't make that nigga wrap up."

I rolled my eyes, and Rizzo just stared out the window. I loved my girl, but I call it as I see it, and that nigga is toxic to her and Tamia if you asked me.

"Lola, I know I fucked up and keep fucking up. I need to leave him alone, and that is why I didn't stay with him, I brought my ass right back home. You would know that if you ever picked up for me. I get what you are saying, but a bitch can't fight him when he starts to touch me. It's been

45

so long that I lose my mind." She tried me, and I shook my head.

"New dick makes you forget a lot of things. Fuck Croy, that dick is beyond used and worn out. You need to focus on you and my niece, to be honest. I love you both too much to see you go down a struggling path that you could have avoided."

I meant that shit. Rizzo was walking right into the devil's den.

"I wish I could move out of the hood and away from his grasp, but this chump change we are making here will not afford me that. I need to find another job and soon," Rizzo tried to move off the subject, but I was on it.

"Then hop on *Indeed.com* when you get off then, but for now, I need to make sure you are done with this nigga. If you are serious, I will find a way to get you all of that. You know Truth don't like his ass, so it's nothing for him to make sure you get away from him."

Truth didn't mingle with my girls or have a bond with them. Truth would speak and get on with his business. He wasn't for the gossiping.

"Fine damn, you don't have to be so fucking harsh. I was already on my fuck Croy campaign anyway."

"Yeah, well, don't fuck him because you are fucking for the wrong cause," I joked, and Rizzo flipped me off.

I finally explained that Tamiko was off, and Rizzo told me she didn't have Tamia until the weekend. Since it was only Wednesday, we planned to try to hit a bar to unwind and eat some good wings, while sipping and letting off steam. When we pulled up to work, my phone rang, so Rizzo assured me she would clock me in while I handled the call. There was no way I was missing this call.

"Good morning," I sang into the phone.

I smiled so hard that my eyes naturally closed, and

wrinkles formed in the corners of my eyes. It was something only I noticed, and I loved it about myself.

"Just what I needed to hear, now I can open my eyes," his deep baritone called out to me, and my body trembled.

"So how did you dial my number if your eyes were closed?" I asked, still beaming.

"When you are the only one I talk to, it's not hard to find you in my call log. You about to clock in, so I just called to say have a good day, and you need to quit like I been saying."

Even though his words pissed me off, I let that shit slide, only because it was him though.

"I like having my own money, but again your offer is nice and still being sat upon. Thank you for calling. I'll ring on my break."

"Text me thirty minutes before so that I can give you some of this dick to finish the shift off strong. You know you're going to be on bitch mode after that lunch rush," he joked, but he was telling nothing but facts.

"You tell no lies. Talk to you later, babe," I cooed.

"Always." I ended the call and got out to start my shift.

Since it was a weekday, and we worked at a highway location near major businesses and companies, our rush was going to start around ten, so I needed to make sure I was ready. After talking to my mystery man, I was on a cloud and ready for two o'clock to come so that I could get this pussy worked!

7

Truth Lee

I was only at my crib for one reason, Tamiko was off, and I wanted to dive face-first into her sweetness. I wasn't about to tell Lola's nosey ass that, especially after going in on her ass about the smell of a nigga in here. Lola had a mouth on her, but I inherited the same, so she wasn't shutting me down in an argument. Tamiko wasn't just a fuck, and I had only been between her legs once, but I couldn't resist another chance.

I had wanted to fuck with Tamiko's ass for a long time, but she was dodging me because Lola's loud mouth ass told her I slang drugs. I had to lie and tell her I was out of the game just to let her accept my date offer. We had only been kicking it for about two months now, but I was feeling her vibe for now. I had bitches, but Tamiko didn't need to know that and neither did Lola. The way the streets would talk, I had to keep to myself on a few things.

It had been an hour since Tamiko was supposed to be here, so I pulled out my phone and shot her a quick text.

Me: *You straight?*

Miko: *Yeah, sorry. They were short at work and called me in, raincheck?*

Me: *Bet.*

Miko: *Don't be like that.*

I placed my phone in my pocket and grabbed my keys. This was one of the reasons I couldn't make Tamiko mine. She always ran to that half-ass job at Taco Bell. Them niggas stayed short-staffed and never did any hiring. I was growing tired of her dodging me to go into that mold infested place. On top of everything, their manager was racist as fuck and worked them all to the bone for a measly $7.75 per hour. I never knocked their hustle, but they were all too grown for the shit.

Lola Rizzo and Tamiko were smart enough to run their own business, but they put that time into that fast food shit. Since Tamiko wanted to tend to them, I headed over to my ex's crib to see what's up. As if Orion could feel where I was headed, my phone rang, and it was him.

"Yo," I answered, enjoying smooth traffic.

"Not shit, what the fuck you getting into right now?" Orion sounded like something was up, so I pulled over so I could focus on his tone.

"Nothing major, you need me?" I asked, and Orion told me how the beef Croy fueled had taken a turn for the worse. It was now at our back door.

"Now, they think we had something to do with it. Even though we clean on their accusations, I want to make sure they don't feel the need to make anymore," Orion huffed, and I nodded my head.

"Facts. We need to handle that little brother of yours, man. Croy is becoming bad for business, and I can't let him or anyone else come in between me and my money."

I meant every word. I know Orion and Croy were brothers, but Croy was a hothead that would get us jammed up. The only reason he was still making money with us was because his father supplied the purest cocaine for us. He wasn't even Orion's father, but you could tell that Orion was his favorite.

"Man, I don't even try with that nigga anymore. All this female drama he stays in keeps me away from his ass. Croy is going to learn, and his daddy is going to have to teach him that. Speaking of Ro, we gotta meet up with him and explain this shit down to him. That nigga ain't feeling this attention we are getting on our spots."

I knew that shit would get to Ro, but I was hoping that he would put two and two together and figure out his seed was the cause of all of this. Croy started beef with the east and west side of the 'Boro, by fucking on their cousin and making she think he was a west side nigga. Somehow, she saw a picture of him, and word got out he ran with us, and now they on our ass. I wasn't worried about an east side nigga. I was worldwide with mine, and if they stepped to me, I would show them why.

"Shit set that shit up and hit me with the location. I gotta handle something, and then I'll be at the barber's for a shape-up, so meet me there," I said, and Orion agreed.

I wasn't going to the barbershop, but instead to a little chick Leni that we fuck with place. We stashed our money there, and I needed to take some off to make sure rent was paid, and Tamiko got this Cardi B Fashion Nova line she keeps crying about. Since we didn't need that shit to be raided, we called it the barbershop and only went when we needed to get some money cleaned.

Leni's twin sister Lenox cleaned the money for us, using some of her friends to spend the cash at stores and going to other stores to get refunds. The shit was on them if they got caught, but Lenox paid them enough to make sure they ate well while they were laying down.

I had no issues out of Lenox or Leni until I fucked up and fucked them both. It wasn't even my fault, I thought I was fucking Leni twice in one day, but she swears I should know her body. After that, Orion was able to make it strictly business for Leni and me, but Lenox hopped on the dick with ease when I called. I think Leni knew because lately, she had been pure evil. Lenox was the ex I was referring to. I couldn't shake shorty if I wanted to, and with Tamiko being childish as fuck, I had to get my nut somewhere.

I pulled up to her five-bedroom house and got out. I loved the way Lenox kept her grass trimmed and her flowers in her garden based on the year. Nothing had changed with this girl, and I shook my head at the thought. I knocked, and she opened the door with nothing on. I licked my lips at the sight in front of me. Lenox was very comfortable with her body, so worrying about her neighbors seeing was the furthest thing from her mind right now.

"I guess your little young bitch was busy, huh? Leave that hoe alone and come get with this stallion." Lenox rubbed the top of her pussy, at the same time pulling me into her home.

Lenox wasted no time trying to rip my clothes from my body, but I grabbed her hands and stopped her. She wasn't about to fuck up my gear trying to get to this dick. She needed to chill the fuck out. I picked Lenox up and carried her upstairs to her bedroom, where I laid her down and removed my clothes. Lenox flipped over and assumed the doggy style position like I loved. Lenox and Leni were fucking gorgeous, from their short fairy cuts to their thick ass hips, thighs, and ass. They were both short and always thought to be weak but had bodied plenty of niggas for thinking wrong.

I looked over Lenox's chocolate skin, and something about it made me hard as fuck. I had a thing for chocolate girls, maybe it was from my mother's side, but I needed to be inside Lenox. I eased into her and Lenox began to throw it back, fucking up my rhythm. I couldn't stop her though. The way Lenox worked her hips while she threw it back was making it harder to hold back this nut.

"Fuck! I needed this, daddy. Don't cum yet!" she moaned, and I just slapped her on the ass.

I pushed her face into the pillows and took charge. I grabbed her arms with one hand and fucked the shit out of Lenox. From the way her pussy was clamped over my dick, I knew Lenox was losing her mind. I could feel myself about to nut, so I pulled out and came all over Lenox's ass, back, and lastly, her hair. Lenox's body shook as she came fingering herself in the same position. I sat back and watched because Lenox had one of the prettiest pussies that I had ever laid eyes on.

"Shit, Truth! You came in my fucking hair, nigga?" Lenox yelled, and I laughed a little while heading for her bathroom. I needed to shower, but Lenox was on my heels.

"I know you hear me, you mute motherfucker! Damn, I know we just fucking, but you don't disrespect me like this!" Lenox pointed at the semen drying on her hair.

I shook my head, looking her up and down, making my dick stiffen.

"You needed something to make that shit grow. Come on, man. You talking all that shit. Let me fuck you in the shower." I smiled, and Lenox fell right into my trap. I knew I should have showered and gone to her sister's crib, but I had to feel her one more time before I left, and it was well worth it.

FINALLY, at the barbershop and waiting for Orion, I decide to go ahead in. As soon as my boots hit the last step, the screen door flew open, and Leni rushed out, popping more shit than a little bit. Leni stayed in Harriston Homes across from Rizzo, but they didn't fuck with each other. There was no beef. Rizzo just didn't speak, and Leni wasn't paid to be social.

"You dirty dick chink ass fucker! You still fucking my sister ain't you, Truth?" Leni yelled, and I pushed her ass into the house because the nosey ass neighbors were all ready for a good show in this heat. Once we were inside, Leni continued to go off on me like I was her nigga. She'd cut me off from the pussy.

"How can you fuck my sister after fucking with me, Truth? Then to add insult to injury, you still fucking her and doing her just as dirty. You foul as fuck, and I will only be doing business with Orion. Get the fuck out, Truth!" Leni pointed to the door behind me to show me she meant business, but I paid her, not the other way around.

I sat down and pulled my phone out to text Tamiko, but Leni was mugging me so hard that I moved it over to look at her. I knew she was mad about me fucking with Lenox on the low, but that shit was her own fault. I wasn't dealing with her bullshit, so if she was on this, I would stay in my phone. Orion walked in without knocking and looked us both up and down before shaking his head.

"You two need to hash that beef shit out. What you got for us, Leni?" Orion asked, putting his phone up and throwing a bag of cash on the wooded table Leni had in her dining room.

Leni rolled her eyes at me and walked over to grab the bag and then over to where Orion stood.

"I don't have shit for your little mute right hand, but I have four bags in the back for you, Orion. You need to get this joke of a nigga out of my shit before I go out there and fuck his wheels up," Leni said, and I took that as my cue. Leni had fucked up an old car of mine, and I knew she was good for it.

"Leni, you need to chill the fuck out touching people's shit! I don't say shit because there is nothing to say. In your eyes, I will never be shit, but you cut me off, Lenox didn't. You need to take that shit up with her. When it comes to business, you need to separate the two."

I went to go and grab my two bags, and Orion stepped in to go and get them. Leni took that as her time to remove shit from her chest.

"You knew my sister is tatted up Truth, so there is no way you got the two of us confused with the other! You played me and tried to use the twin card for why you fucked up. You were foul and still can't admit to it. You right, I am hurting from that shit, and business is business. You got it Truth, but know you missed out on a good thing fucking me over."

Leni moved from around me and snatched her cigarettes from the coffee table. I watched her storm out of the house, but I followed her sneaky ass. I knew Orion would get my money while I watched this spiteful hoe. I should have been on the way to Tamiko, but I had shit to handle with Orion, so I chilled until he was done, ignoring Leni's mean mug the whole time.

8

Tamiko Lyons

"So, you not coming out with us?" Lola asked, fixing her lip gloss in her car mirror as we smoked a blunt on our break.

I rolled my eyes, still waiting for Truth to respond to me about where the fuck his ass was. I had been fucking with Truth for a little minute, but he was too much of a hoe to be my main thing. Plus, Lola would kill us both and smack me silly for fucking with his hoe ass. I couldn't stop if I wanted to though, Truth wasn't rough or mean to me. He took his time with me. I could talk to him more than I could my girls because my mindset was different.

"I told you I have shit to do. If you can wait an hour or two for me, then I'm down, but like I said, I got shit to do," I countered, and Lola looked back at me while Rizzo passed the blunt.

"I have an order. I'll be right back."

Rizzo jumped out, and we heard her taking the order while she walked into the store. I still didn't know how Rizzo could take three orders from outside and walk in, getting each order right and getting them out in time.

Lola cleared her throat, and I looked at her like she was sick or something.

"You good up there?" I joked, and she smacked my knee.

"I found your draws in Truth's room this morning. You wouldn't be fucking my brother, would you?" she asked, and I knew my face would have been beet red if I wasn't dark toned.

"Would it be a bad thing?" I asked, and Lola frowned her face up and nodded.

"Tamiko, now you know my brother is a hoe, and he has plenty of pussy walking in and out of our house. Why would you even do that to yourself? I love you and think you would be perfect for Truth's ass, but I can't lose a best friend behind his shit. I'll beat his ass and then yours for trying to leave me alone because of his mess." Lola smiled, and I smiled back.

"Don't worry. I got me when it comes to this heart thing. Truth is a hoe, and I know this, but he had calmed down since fucking with me." I smiled with certainty, but the look Lola gave before turning around had me questioning if I could be this certain. "What?" I asked because she knew more than she was willing to say.

"Truth will always be Truth. He ain't slowed down with shit. Truth just doesn't bring them home."

Lola put the blunt out and got out the car. I felt so hot I didn't know if I could finish my fucking shift. Since this was overtime, I called after Lola to clock me out. I went to my car and pulled out, hitting the highway. Truth had me fucked up if he was out here fucking anything that walks while dipping in this pussy.

Lola wasn't trying to snitch on her brother, and I understood that, but I was happy she had kept it a buck with me. I never sped so fast until today, and then I wondered why I was even doing this much. If Truth wanted to play this game, then game on. I was good at leaving a nigga alone, and Truth was going to get the first lesson. Instead of going to him, I went to get Tamia and took her for ice cream while I waited for the girls to get off. Fuck it. I was going to fuck it up with my bitches and find some new dick to cry about.

———

FINALLY, after hours of chocolate ice cream and playing at the park, I took Tamia back to Mama Rose's house and went to meet up with Rizzo and Lola. Lola had already filled Rizzo in, to no surprise, but I had to give them both all the tea, and it surprised them both.

"Damn, my brother never told me any of that." Lola put her head down.

"Truth always wants to be strong for you because every girl needs their mother, but he was fucked up behind it too. Seeing her walk out on you two fucked up how he looked at women for a while. He claims until he met me, but we know he is bullshitting."

I chuckle, but neither of them joins in. Rizzo and Lola share a look, but I wave it off.

"So, where are we going?" I asked, getting up and grabbing a bottle of Stella Rosa and three wine glasses.

"I was thinking Limelight, or One17, I heard they have the best nightlife parties," Rizzo said, filling her damn glass up.

"I'm down with One17. Limelight has all the hoes in there and no niggas. I'll be damned if I get fucked over by a stud again." I fell out with Rizzo listening to Lola's dumb ass.

"It was not that bad, and she was cute as fuck!" I chimed in, and Lola gave me an evil glare.

"Yeah, without a dick, I need all that powerful muscle in my life." I shook my head, laughing.

Since Lola had taken care of our outfits with her sick sewing talents, I started on our hair. Lola wanted her bone straight, and as easy as that seemed, I had a thick ass head of hair to tame. Rizzo had her twist out setting, so she was good, but wanted me to beat her face, and that I did with ease. Rizzo didn't need much makeup, so I just applied her some Mink Lashes from Garden of Minks collection and some lip gloss. After fixing her eye shadow and eyebrows, she was done.

I did the same and started on Lola's hair. Midway through her hair, Truth began to blow my phone up. I placed him on the block list because I was done fucking with his lying ass. I was willing to let Truth do him because he wasn't my nigga, but I asked him not to lie about it and keep his dick wrapped up. Here he was being Mr. Community Dick.

"Don't ignore his ass. You might as well tell him you done," Lola said while scrolling Facebook.

"Fuck him, he can call another bitch," I countered, meaning it. If I wasn't enough for Truth, then so be it, I wasn't begging.

"You know he will."

Lola was pissing me off. I mushed her head and left the room. I could hear her asking Rizzo what she did, but it wasn't even her. I knew Truth would call the next bitch, but it was my fault for falling for his ass. Either way, I didn't need to hear shit bout Truth and nothing bitch. Something about it made my head hurt, and my blood boil.

"You know she ain't mean shit by it." Rizzo walked up on me in the kitchen while I drank some water. I shrugged.

"It's cool. I just wish this nigga would stop playing with me. Lola's good, that's my bitch either way it goes. I shouldn't have ever fucked his ass."

"This is true, but if you were something special to Truth, he will see what he's lost. Tonight, it's about us. Let's go turn up!" Lola said, and I tried my best to be in the same mood.

———

ONCE WE WERE ALL DONE, we headed out and got in free thanks to Lola knowing the bouncer. One17 had all the dope boys out flossing and throwing money. I knew it had to be a club full of coke heads if they are balling out like this tonight. We found a table and waited for Lola to come back with our first round of drinks. Rizzo and I scoped out the scene while twirling our hips to "Please Me" by Cardi B and Bruno Mars. Bitches had these niggas almost fucking on the floor. It was crazy in here tonight. They didn't give a fuck what tricks they popped out on the dance floor for everyone to see.

"Oh shit, let's go find, Lola," Rizzo said, but I had to turn to see what the fuck she peeped that I hadn't.

As soon as I looked, I wished I hadn't. Truth was getting twerked on by some chick in his VIP section. My blood was boiling as our eyes met, and he gave this sinister grin.

"Damn, who is that beside him?" Rizzo asked just as Lola got back.

"Girl that's Orion sexy ass, but—"

I didn't even get the rest because I was on my way to their section. Truth had been blowing me up all day and night just to be in another bitch face in the club, not to mention shorty looked like she was comfortable as hell to be sitting on his lap kissing his ear and shit. Truth thought I was a goody-two-shoes, but that was because I wanted him to, I had to show him I was nothing to play with.

On the way to his section, I grabbed an Ace of Spades bottle and smoothly walked up on them. The security looked me up and down before letting me in. Once inside, Rizzo and Lola circled the girl, and she let out a laugh with her homegirls she was with who was trying too hard to be known.

"What the fuck is this? Isn't this your sister, babe?" she asked, and I crooked my neck at Truth.

"Babe? Damn, didn't know y'all were all of that when you were feasting on Phat Momma, shiiiid. I see you, Truth." I smirked, replacing the slick smile he once had.

Truth just shook his head, and I expected that from his ass. Truth wouldn't buck up for shit, so let me give him some motivation. I crashed the bottle over shorty head and watched her bottle topple over to the floor. The two minions with her tried to come for us, but Lola knocked one in the throat, and Rizzo was giving the other more work than the unemployment office.

Truth jumped up and yoked me up, trying to move me out of the club. I went to swinging on his ass. I was going in on his ass until I saw the Orion dude snatch Rizzo up from her waist, and some other guy carrying Lola the other way talking shit in her ears. I tried to get to Rizzo because we ain't know this nigga for him to be touching her, but Truth grabbed my hair and yanked me out the club.

"Bitch, I will find your ass. Stay looking, hoe!" I heard the girl yell once the music stopped from our fight.

"No need, Harriston Homes bitch!" I yelled back, but Truth gripped tighter on my hair, shutting me up.

I knew I had pissed him off when he threw me into the

car and sped off without another word. When I saw he was leaving the hood, I knew we were going to his condo, but I didn't even want to be around him. Truth wanted me to show my ass tonight, and that's exactly what I did. If he was mad, then he could blame the head in his pants. I leaned over and waited out the ride. Truth could fuck himself tonight for all I cared.

9

Rizzo

I didn't know who this nigga was or why he was carrying me to his car, but I wasn't going anywhere with him. Too many women were raped and sold away from just leaving with random niggas. It wouldn't be me. Once he got me in, I was kicking the door to get out, and he wore the biggest mean mug on his face. Fine and all, Orion would catch these hands if he tried me.

"Yo, chill the fuck out, kicking my car and shit. On your income, you can't afford to fix shit in here!" he boomed, and I placed my feet down immediately and rolled my eyes.

"You should have minded your business and left me on my way. You can let me out though," I said, and she shook his head before starting his car up and zooming out of the hood. I looked at this nigga like he was crazy in the head.

We pulled up to some fresh ass condos that I had only heard about from Tamiko and Lola. I always wanted to live here, but my girls said think bigger, and I had. Orion parked his car and got out, waiting for me to do the same. I didn't know him, and I wasn't moving. I could see him getting upset, and it was sexy as fuck, but I had to keep my game face on.

"Yo, ma, I will drag you out my shit. Stop fucking with me. You done fucked up my night enough. Come the fuck on!" His voice elevated, and I rolled my eyes and got out.

I saw Tamiko walk out, swatting Truth's hand from her waist, so I walked over to where they were.

"Why this nigga kidnapped me, bitch? You okay?" I asked, eyeing Truth, who wore a smirk on his face.

"Yeah, we need to call Lola and get home. I am not staying with this nigga?" Tamiko flipped Truth the bird, and he blew her a kiss.

"Next time call that bitch an Uber. I don't have the temper for her mouth," Orion said, and I whipped my head into his direction.

"Would you allow your daughter to go with a stranger, nigga? I doubt it, so fuck out of here with that. Your big fine ass will get fucked up tonight."

I walked up to him, but Tamiko grabbed me, and Orion smirked. I wanted to slap that smirk right off his face, but a car pulling in fast as hell startled us.

When Lola jumped out, I noticed Orion place his arm back to his side. Thank God, he was packing though.

"JB, you are not my fucking daddy nigga! Truth, take the girls and me home now!" Lola yelled, walking up on us. Lola's lipstick was smudged, and her dress wasn't fitting the way it was when we left, but I held tight to the thought for a later time.

"Get your cry baby ass in the car. You too, Rizzo! Tamiko, come here before you go."

Truth reached out for Tamiko, but she yanked back and followed us to the car. While they chopped it up, we did the same thing.

"He swears he thinks he got me stuck on stupid or

something. I bet he will be with that bitch again tonight." Tamiko shook her head and looked out the window.

"Fuck him. Make him wish he never fucked around on you, sis. Orion got me fucked up calling me out of my name. Croy tries the same shit and gets decked in the mouth, and so can his big ass."

I eyed Orion and loved how I could see his muscles as he dapped Truth up. Orion was milk chocolate with a full beard. Orion's huge muscles captivated me the most. It had me thinking about getting scooped up by them.

"Lola! Get the fuck out the car!" we heard, and Truth whipped his neck in the direction of some tall, fine chocolate man walked over in a nice ass suit and opened Lola's door. If this was the man making her stand us up, then I was all for it. Truth walked up on him, and his mug let me know it was nothing good about to happen. To all our surprise, the dude turned smoothly and looked over Truth's head, stopping him in his tracks.

"Something over here pays your bills?" he asked, finally looking down at Truth.

"Fuck all that, brah. That's my sister, so it anything when it comes to that one. Why the fuck you are yelling at her like that?" Truth asked, and dude laughed.

"Lola, you want to explain to your brother who I am?" He moved so that she could look up at Truth, and the confusion was evident on everyone but Truth.

"You are fucking JB, Lola?" he asked, and she nodded.

Truth hauled off and slapped fire from her ass, and all hell broke out. JB tried to catch Lola, but her long legs jumped up and onto Truth, and they were tussling. Tamiko was trying to get her down and ended up falling. I said fuck it. I wasn't getting hurt between those two nut cases. I helped Tamiko up, and JB and Orion broke them two up while we looked on.

"Truth, you will never see me again nigga! How are you going to go off on this man for yelling at me and you put your fucking hands on me? Nigga, fuck you, and you better hope I can forget about this shit, pussy ass nigga!" Lola yelled while JB carried her red face off to his car.

Truth didn't say shit but turned and stormed to his condo. Tamiko shook from my grasp and went after him, leaving me alone again with this damn Orion.

"Can you please just take me home?" I asked, and he nodded, wiping his head and pulling his keys from his pocket. This was too much for one night. I was ready to get in my bed and get some sleep. For some reason, Orion was being nicer with the car ride home, but I was happy because I couldn't take anything else negative in my life right now. Croy began to call me, but I ignored it and tried to spark a conversation with Orion.

"So, are you always rude as fuck when you first meet someone?" I asked, and he chuckled.

"See, and here I thought we would have a nice ride. I wasn't being rude. I was doing what was asked. Truth is the homie, and when y'all started to fuck them girls up, we all had one to carry out. You were mine." Orion licked his lips after he said mine, and I bit my bottom lip.

Orion had some sexy ass teeth. This man couldn't be from Greensboro. We just didn't breed these types. I looked at his hand and saw there was no wedding band. That was perfect.

"It wasn't like that, but given the situation, you were rude. Tell me something, when you're upset, do you want to hear calm down?" I asked, turning to him, and she smirked.

"Nah, and if you ever tried it, I would still shut your ass down. It's always the cute ones with all the fucking mouth," Orion said, and I rolled my eyes.

So, he thinks I'm cute. Play it cool, Rizzo.

"I just don't play about my best friends, period. I am sure you are the same way with Truth's hoe ass. I couldn't believe he brought that girl in the club and made sure Tamiko saw him." I shook my head, thinking about how pissed off Tamiko was. Truth was dead ass wrong for that, but after tonight, I knew it wouldn't happen again.

"I understand why you're upset, but that really isn't your business. You look like you have a good head on your shoulders if you contain your mouth, but you seem cool. What Truth and your homegirl do is on them. You gotta worry about yourself, ma."

Orion looked at me and licked his lips again before shaking his head.

"Why you keep doing that? Speak your mind," I said, and he chuckled again.

"You look like trouble, but on everything I love, I want to fuck with you light bright," Orion said, and I looked out the window to see he was already in Harriston Homes. I showed him how to get to my building, and he parked.

"Thanks for the ride. Trouble is leaving the building." I smiled and gathered my stuff to go into the house. When Orion got out too, I looked back, confused. "Aht aht, what are you doing?" I asked with a confused looked.

"Walking you in, ma. You in the hood, and your door is cracked open. I just want to make sure you good."

I couldn't even say no because Orion grabbed my arm gently and walked me to my doorstep. Easing the door open, Orion pulled his gun from behind his back. I tried to hit the lights, but nothing was coming on. I turned my phone's flashlight on, and sure enough, someone had torn my entire crib apart. I was livid and rushed upstairs to make sure they didn't take my stash.

I had been saving up since Tamia was born to have my

own crib, and the goal was for it to come from just me. Croy had been financing me for so long, and I knew a time would come where I was sick of his back and forth shit. I had saved up twenty grand, and for me, that wasn't enough. I wanted to be an author, and I needed to be able to quit my job and live off that once I did. I knew writing wouldn't just take off overnight, so I wanted to make sure Tamia didn't lack for shit when I did pick up and leave. But, like greyhounds, the dope fiends found my stash and even took my baby brand new game system.

"Damn, look, I don't think you need to stay here tonight, plus it looks like your lights have been cut off," Orion said from behind me, and I shook my head.

Croy usually took care of that, and since I had been dodging him, I guess it slipped his mind. Had I not been robbed, I would have the money to put on my fucking bill. I was so furious that I hopped up and moved past Orion to my room. I packed as much as I could with my flashlight and Orion's.

"Where you going to go, shorty?" he asked, and even though I knew Orion meant well by his question, I was pissed and didn't have time for the questions, especially when I hadn't answered them my damn self.

"I have no fucking clue. I will probably go to my mother's until my lights are back on. I'll come back tomorrow to clean the place up. There is no need to file a claim. I won't get any of the shit back. My shit is getting smoked up as we speak, I am sure of it."

I suddenly plop right in the middle of clothes everywhere. I couldn't see Orion because of the light from his phone, but I saw his hand extend out to mine.

"Just a minor setback. You can stay out in my condo until you get straight, and I'll take you to get your shorty if you need to. I don't think you should stay here by yourself, and you seem down about having to go to your dukes' crib."

I brushed myself off and turned my camera to Orion's face. Orion had full juicy lips, but his eyes were so honest and sweet. It made it hard to believe he ran the streets as Lola said.

"Thanks, but I will be fine at my mother's."

Orion nodded and grabbed my bags, and carried down my staircase.

I knew I should have taken the offer, but I wanted to be with family right now. I didn't want to be alone at all at this moment. I know it was only crackheads, but I didn't feel safe for some reason.

When we got to my mother's, Orion walked me to the door with my bags. My mother came to the door and looked him up and down.

"Is everything okay, Rizzo?" she asked, looking at Orion.

"Yes mama, I didn't pay my light bill, so I need to stay here. Plus, someone broke in and took just about everything of value that I own. This is Orion, a friend of Truth, Lola's brother. He had been a huge help today, but I'll explain more inside. Is daddy home?" I asked, and she nodded, letting us in.

Orion put the bags down and spoke properly before leaving. I watched him walk out the door and to his car, I prayed that I ran into him again, but then again, that wouldn't be good. I needed to focus on me, and after tonight, getting the fuck from out of Harriston Homes Apartments as well.

I sat back and drank tea while I ran everything down to my mother. I was tired, and so was she because after our talk, we both retired to bed. Orion was heavy on my mind.

10

Orion Lahey

I drove back to my spot with Rizzo on my mind. Shorty was a firecracker, but nothing I hadn't dealt with. I loved how she rode for her girls, but I wish she saw what I see and what she was exemplifying for her daughter. That it is never okay for a female of such statures to lower herself for a man. Don't get me wrong, Truth is the homie, and I was down for him the long way, but he was wrong for fucking with Lenox right in front of Rizzo's friend. It wasn't my issue, so I hoped they figured that shit out. If it didn't fuck with my operation, then I was good.

Before I could make it home, my brother Croy was calling me back-to-back. I didn't fuck with him like that because Croy was messy and never thought strategically about anything. When in the streets, you always had to be ten moves ahead of everyone else. Truth was quiet, but his moves made more noise, and that's why I fucked with him. Croy had started a beef trying to cancel out one side of town and now had both sides after our organization. Shit wasn't sitting right with JB, nor Faheem.

"Yo, this better be you saying you found a viable solution to this fucked up predicament you put us in," I answered, and Croy's bitch ass laughed into the phone.

"Bro, take the thong out your ass. Meet me at the spot."

This nigga hung up, and I had to take a few deep breaths since I was still driving, but Croy was poking a nerve. This nigga thought he was running shit, and it was the other way around. Brother or not, respect me, nigga! Truth understood his position and played his role. There was loyalty between Truth and me. The only bond between Croy and I was the blood of our mother.

Croy didn't fuck with me or respect me because he felt his pops rocked with me more than him. Honestly, he did, and I told him about that shit. I never liked how favored me over his own seed, and Croy always saw it. I used to try to make the nigga feel better, but that shit died when he stole from me when I turned eighteen. Croy took the party luck box that was filled with nothing but hundreds. I found the empty box behind his bed like a pussy nigga. When Farooq said leave him, I was pissed until Croy came home fucked up one day, and his father said nothing about it. Our mother, Marissa, on the other hand, was ready to go to war for her baby, as she should have been.

I made my way to the spot, and Croy was standing outside looking like some crack head who found a lick to hit. I got out and sparked a blunt to get myself ready for what he was bringing this time.

"What's up?" I asked, and he mugged me.

"You don't have to sound like I pulled you out of some pussy nigga, damn. I got one of the niggas that hit us tied up in there. I figured you would want answers on how they were moving," Croy said, and my eyes lit up.

Shit, for once, maybe my brother got something right.

I dapped Croy up and gave him a head nod before

walking into the spot. It smelled as usual, but when I saw the young boy tied up with a bullet in his head, I was enraged. I turned and looked at Croy with such disgust.

"What the fuck, Croy? How the fuck are we going to get anything from the nigga if he's dead?" I asked, smacking Croy upside the head.

I paced the floor because now we were short on information. I needed to know how hard these niggas were coming. I wasn't scared, but I liked to be prepared. I needed to go and see Leni again and get some moves in play. I look back at Croy as he starts to go off.

"Yo, I did what the fuck I thought was right. He told me everything. Trust a nigga for once," he said, and I walked up on him.

"What did he say then nigga, huh? Give me that shit word for word on your life." I mugged Croy, and I was heaving, trying to keep from knocking him on his ass.

"Get the fuck out my face, O!" Croy stepped forward, pushing his chest out and shit. Before his nose could even graze mine, I had my gun at Croy's temple, safety off.

"Make your move, nigga. I told you to start thinking before you move. What did he say and think before you give me the wrong information."

I was livid, and the way Croy tried to eye my gun with his peripheral vision, I knew he knew what the fuck was up. Croy ran that shit down for me, and I smacked him with my gun knocking him out. I left his ass to sleep right where he laid. He needed to think about that shit for a little minute.

I went to my condo and laid out, thinking about how a nice phat ass would be nice to rub after the stressful day I'd had. Sleep came soon after.

I WOKE up and washed my balls before getting laced and headed out to Leni's crib. I knew she cleaned money for a few west and east side niggas, so if anyone knew something, it was going to be Leni's ass. Leni used to be feeling a nigga, but after she fucked Truth, I didn't look at her the same. It sounds shallow, but shorty was now used.

When I walked in, Leni was ready to tear me a new asshole.

"I know your ass isn't in my shit after you let them bitches bust my sister's head open! She had to get sixteen stitches on her face and then surgery to repair her face after it heals! What the fuck, O?" Leni's small frame walked up on me, and I looked down at her like she had lost her mind.

"What the fuck does that have to do with me? Your sister was running her mouth to some unknowns, and we the reason they didn't do any more damage." Leni rolled her eyes but didn't move an inch.

"Orion, we have been working with you for years and always stayed loyal. All I'm saying is someone should have had Lenox back, and if I were there, it wouldn't have gone down like that. I know how you and your boys get down, but put some respect on my sister and me. Now, what's your business for coming here?" Leni turned and walked back to her couch, sparking a pre-rolled blunt in the process.

"I need info on those west side and east side boys. I know you clean money for them too, and that's no issue, but we have beef now, and I need to know how they are moving against us," I said, sitting a stack of cash on the table. Leni looked at the money and laughed, choking on the smoke she had just inhaled.

"You're really insulting me, and after everything I just

let come out my mouth." Leni shook her head but broke it down to me.

The east side had a meeting with us in two days, and they were going to let them west side niggas in on some ambush type of shit. The only issue would be that my niggas and I would be waiting.

"Was that so hard?" I asked, and Leni rolled her eyes.

"It actually was, especially when you don't know if the person you are being so loyal to is loyal to you." Leni eyed me, and I had to know what she meant by that.

"What the fuck is that shit you on, Leni?"

"I'm saying O, you come in here for information but keeping it slick when it comes to my sister. If that were Croy's bitch ass, you would have expected me to move different, wouldn't you?" she asked, and I shook my head.

"Tuh, either way, it was foul. Truth knew his little chick would be in there, and he set my sister up. Now you are sitting here asking me for a lifeline for that same man. I looked at you like a brother, and you sitting here like how I feel don't matter. Not once have I ever come at you like this, Orion, but I need you to leave. I gave you what you asked for, but I need you out of my house right now."

Leni walked over to her door and opened it for me. I had never pissed her off to where Leni had to kick a nigga out, but I had shit to do, so I didn't argue.

I left out and called Truth as I got inside my car. I knew that the meeting was going to be interesting, but not as juicy as this. Truth answered and sounded still pissed off.

"Yo?"

"I'm on the way, cheer up snowflake," I joked and hung up, making my way over to his condo.

Since I knew Tamiko stayed over, I was cautious when using my key to get in, but to my surprise, all that was there was Truth, looking stressed the fuck out. Truth was in the same clothes from last night and looked as if he hadn't slept a wink all night. When I turned the lights on, I just knew this nigga had been crying all night. Empty bottles of liquor were sprawled all over the ground, and it was evident then that Truth was smacked.

"What the fuck, Truth?" I asked, picking the bottles up from a chair and sitting down.

"Nigga, don't come in here jumping in my business. Bust that info down for me so I can go back to my vibes alone." Truth sat up and took a swig of his Patrón.

I ran everything down to him and got up to leave.

"What the fuck? So, now you don't want my input on how we take these niggas down?" he asked, and I shook my head.

"I'm giving you your vibe back, nigga. I got shit to handle, so if you in your feelings, I'm leaving your ass there." I turned and walked out the door.

I didn't have time for this shit, and that was why I didn't fuck around with bird ass females. The loud ass shit was a turnoff and always in some drama was a no-go. I needed a female with character and ambition, someone who had morals about herself, and if she needed to, she could handle herself. Instead of working with Truth to get these niggas, I sent out a mass message for a meeting and headed back to the spot to handle it. Croy might want to show up with his head on his shoulder.

11

Rizzo

I was tired as fuck trying to get my house back together as best as I could. I couldn't believe I had been robbed, and they trashed my shit in the process. I couldn't let Tamia come home and see this, my baby was too dramatic and probably wouldn't sleep for weeks. Momma said she was fine there, so Lola and Tamiko were here helping me while we talked about last night.

I hadn't told them about riding back with Orion because they had been going on and on about their night, and it sounded more important anyway. I just sat back and gave advice when I could while ignoring Croy as he called my phone. I should have been put this nigga on the block list, but he had to be in touch with Tamia somehow.

"Truth is a whole bitch! I know you love his dirty draws, but fuck him. You better keep his weak ass away from me, Tamiko!" Lola went off. I knew she was hurt by what happened, but Tamiko had nothing to do with their little sibling war.

"That's not fair. He disrespected her last night, too, if

you have forgotten," I countered. Lola wrinkled her brows, looking at Tamiko.

"Who were them bitches anyway? You could tell the bitch you hit only hung with the other two to make sure she caught all the niggas." Lola laughed, and I laughed with her, but Tamiko shook her head.

"I have no idea because I never got a real answer as to why shit even went down the way it did. Truth had always said he could talk to me, and he only fucked with other bitches when I wasn't available."

Lola and I looked at each other and then back at Tamiko as if she grew two more heads.

"First off, I know I was dumb for accepting that, and I asked him to stop, which he swore he would. Truth listened to everything I would say and always had great advice. When I was thinking about leaving momma's house because she was drinking too much for me, Truth advised that I talk to her and let her in on how it was affecting me. Same here, so many nights I stayed up and listened to him tell me stories about your mother and his relationship, I hurt for this man, and this is what I get. A huge dick slap to the face, no spit."

Tamiko had Lola and me laughing, and we didn't mean to.

"Girl, Truth knows he fucked up now. You and I were the best things in his life, and he just lost both. Girl, after last night, I had to leave with JB." Lola rolled her eyes and went back to sweeping up the glass from my mirror being thrown to the ground and shattering.

"What's up with JB?" I asked, and the smile that spread across my best friend's face made Tamiko and me smile too.

"Girl, that's their plug. Truth was mad because he thinks if JB and I don't work out, then that is going to be his plug, and shit will get messy. JB isn't even like that, and I don't plan to ever leave that man alone. JB is also almost thirty, and he just got out about four months ago. That's why I've been so distant," Lola said.

"I swear that nigga is sexy as fuck though. I see you. Now, does JB have a younger brother?" I joked.

"He is an only child, but the streets raised him, and he grew his own family, so I'm sure has someone for you. What about dude from last night?" Lola asked, and I wished she hadn't asked me.

I didn't want to talk about how awkward it was and how turned on he made me.

Before I could answer, there was banging at my door, and it made me jump. Lola pulled a gun from her bag before we went downstairs. Swinging the door wide open, Lola aimed the gun at Croy's head, and he put his hands up.

"Put that little ass shit away, Lola, with your crazy ass!" Croy yelled.

I pulled his ass inside, and he looked around.

"It looks fine to me. Your momma said you were robbed, and they trashed the spot. This looks like it used to, but you moved the couch to beside the window."

I rolled my eyes at Croy.

"What do you need, Croy? I need to finish so that Tamia can come home." I placed my hand on my hips, and Lola lowered her gun.

Tamiko and Lola went upstairs to give us space.

"I came to make sure you were straight," Croy said, and I nodded.

"We good, now you can go," I said, and Croy looked like he was going to protest, but his phone chimed and decided to go.

"This ain't over, Rizzo. We need to talk!" Croy yelled as I closed the door.

Looking over my living room and kitchen, I was proud of the work I put in. My living room looked better, and so did my kitchen. Once we finished my room, I would be able to go and bring Tamia home. I ran upstairs, and these two bitches were in my bed midway through a blunt.

"Damn, you couldn't wait for me, I ain't take that long!" I jumped in the bed and snatched it from Lola.

"Lola was telling me how JB has a few jobs that she thinks we can work for him. It's a cleaning position, but the pay is out of this world. I think we should hop on it," Tamiko said, and I looked over at Lola.

"What would we be cleaning though?" I asked. I was down for whatever at this point to make sure I got Tamia out of this hood. Harriston Homes wouldn't get the best of me. Fuck this ghetto shit.

"It is nothing crazy. He owns a cleaning service, and with his new promotion, he's getting more business and is holding interviews anyway. When he told me how much they made an hour, I was on it. JB didn't want me working for Taco Bell anyway, so this was perfect," Lola said, and I was down for it.

"I'm all for this. I need to get Tamia out of here. I'm going to miss you girls." I frowned, and Tamiko turned to us and gave us that *I have an idea* look.

"If we do this, we can save up and get a house together, maybe outside the hood, bitch!" Tamiko was hype about her idea, and it wasn't a bad idea.

"Yeah, but Tamia is a lot full-time, and both of you have patterns in your life that I would hate to disturb." I would love to follow through, but it wouldn't be fair to put Tamia on them full time like that.

"Girl, the fuck bye. Tamia is our baby as much as she is yours! I think we should and boss up on these niggas," Lola said. I figured we could and make something shake. "JB also gave me his card and told me to get Tamia's shit back, so it looks like mommy was decorating her room for her when she got back and pampering ourselves in the process."

Lola waved the card, and we got hype. This was a blessing because I had been trying to find the words to tell Tamia about all her games and systems that were stolen, down to her iPad. It was going to crush her.

We hurried to finish my room, and all we had to do was put everything we could save that was on my bed, away in its rightful place. I was hoping they had every game that she had before, but if not, I would order them and tell her I fell on them while setting up. Tamia would just be happy with a newly decorated room. Since Tamia had been asking for a dry erase stand board, I knew where to start on the list of things to grab. Once we were done, the girls left to shower before Lola picked us all up and we headed to Wendover for Rooms-To-Go.

I had set up an entire twin room set and got my delivery date. I wanted to replace Tamia's wardrobe since they even took all her fresh shoes that Croy and I had gotten her. I think it hurt me the most because I had worked hard for most of the things in here. Croy bought Tamia the world but always kept it at his crib for her to ask me about.

We walked into Kid's Footlocker, and I saw Tiffiah and her friend talking to the chick from the club last night. I know Tamiko's split shorty's shit, but she looked just fine. Tiffiah looked our way after her friend tapped her and pointed at us.

"I hope that bitch don't try shit today!" Lola spat.

"Shorty looks good for a busted head. She must have a twin," Tamiko said and shrugged them bitches off.

We did that same while going to check out shoes. No sooner than we ask for a pair of shoes, and the attendant goes to get them, the three stooges walk over mugging like they have an issue.

"Are you Tamiko?" shorty asked Tamiko, and she turned, looking the girl up and down.

"Who wants to know?" Tamiko asked, and the girl laughed with Tiffiah and Charnell right behind her.

"I don't see shit funny. We came here to shop, and you bitches starting with us. Now, I'm going to need you to either jump or move the fuck around," I said, looking at all three. I wasn't worried about fucking up this store. Tiffiah was known for stealing, and she would take what I had just bought for my baby.

"Nah, I just wanted to introduce myself. I'm Leni, and the girl you attacked at the club was my twin sister. I've never been one to fight fair, so enjoy, but watch our back." She smirked and walked away, leaving Tiffiah and Charnell looking confused.

"I thought you would beat her ass or something, what the fuck, Leni?" Tiffiah rushed off behind her friend like a thirsty nigga.

"Wait until I tell Truth about these bitches." Tamiko pulled her phone out, and Lola went to stop her.

"Girl fuck him, remember? We will handle her ass because I don't know who the fuck Tiffiah thinks she is fucking with, but she has the wrong one. Let's finish getting our baby straight for this move that's coming," Lola said, and we all calmed down with some retail therapy.

Tiffiah had fucked up getting in between something that had nothing to do with her. Lola was nuts, so I was happy to unleash her on the troll and her Burgan.

12

Tiffiah

Leni had pissed me off, acting like she feared them three bitches. I grew up knowing of Leni and Lenox, the twins who fought niggas and whooped ass and cleaned the best drug dealer's money. They never got caught, but I never knew how they did the shit so clean. So, for Leni to be backing down from Rizzo and her minions, I was surprised. I needed her to make moves.

Since the fight with them three at the fair, Croy had been home every night and was really being a family man. I called off Mack, giving him the name of my old side-piece, who wasn't letting me blackmail him for money. Mack killed his ass and was satisfied, but still begs me to come and be with him. I couldn't leave my family, and since Croy was finally putting us first, Armon was eating it up. Croy had even been spending more time with Nadia, and she was eating it up. I was able to have more free time since I was leaving him with the kids every chance I got.

"Leni! I know you fucking hear me!" I yell in the parking lot, going after Leni.

Charnell wanted to find something to wear, but I

needed in on her plan. If Leni wasn't fucking them up now, then I wanted to know when.

"Who the fuck you yelling at? Tiffiah, I don't fuck with you like that because you messy, and you do nothing but lie on people. This was the first time your information panned out one hundred percent, but that doesn't change anything."

I stepped back, looking confused. I just gave her a gold mine, and she was trashing me?

"What is your point?" I asked, now feeling offended.

"My point is, you pulled me aside to get the digits on my vendor subscription channel. We never got you educated on the products because you saw them bitches and was inching to stir some shit up. Next time you see me, turn and walk away sis, and we good."

Leni walked on to her car, and I scrunched my face up. Who the fuck did she think she was reading me like that? The few people who had walked past snickered, and I turned to go and find Charnell so that we could leave, but I got so pissed I went in search of my car so that I could leave.

It was hot, and I was pissed the fuck off, so finding my car wasn't making it any better. I should have just gone back into the mall to find Charnell, but I just wanted to go home and figure out a way to get Rizzo back. Croy had been on his shit, but I wondered if it was all a joke. Too often, I had to act on the feeling. I went through his phone, and sure enough, he fucked Rizzo, raw at that. Reading how her pussy felt to him and how he hoped he got her pregnant was eating at me every day. Over the last week, I had been eyeing him at dinner, thinking of a way to kill his ass.

Once I found my car, I hopped in and turned the car on, letting my air come one and take over my hot and sweaty body. My phone rang, and it was Charnell, I told her I had to hurry and get the kids from Croy's parents, and she fell for it. Charnell said she would catch the bus home, and I pulled off to really go and get my babies.

I wanted to see if Orion's sexy ass was there. It was something about him that made me want to leave the little brother and fuck on the big brother. Orion just walked with power, and his entire being demanded respect.

I remember watching him fuck this girl in his old bedroom one time. I came so hard as they fucked. I thought he caught me because I couldn't contain my moans, and if Croy hadn't called me, I would have come two more times. Orion looked like he would leave me crying for his massive dick. The way he dominated that girl made my clit jump. Orion never gave me the time of day literally. He never spoke to me nor looked at me. It was as if I wasn't there when we were in the same room, and that's why I didn't fuck with him either.

When I got to Croy's parents' house, Armon and Nadia were lying in the yard, so I got out smiling to join them. I could see the displeasure when Marissa saw me pull up, but she would be okay. Bitch ass Marissa was mad because she couldn't make her son leave me alone. I loved to play my role, and I rubbed it in whenever I could.

"Hey, ma." I smiled, and she weakly did the same.

"Afternoon Tiffiah, I have them all ready to go. I put Armon some clothes in his bag and some games his Paw-Paw bought him. Bring them by tomorrow if you have plans and just call before you come this time," she said, and I knew she was being funny to me, but I didn't like the way she rushed me off. I was the mother of her grandchildren, and I needed some support from this family.

"I thought I would stay and speak with you about your

son." I threw Nadia on my hip, and Marissa looked like she was trying to hold it in.

"Tiffiah, I mean you no harm, but I don't agree with how you treat my son, nor how you carry yourself. Please take my grandson and his sister home and off my property."

Marissa didn't even wait for me to respond. She made some wave motion, and I saw two guards coming our way from the front of the house and two from the side post around their land. I took my kids to the car because I didn't need to die behind trying to be accepted. Marissa and everyone else was going to wish they treated me with some sense.

13

Croy

I had been chilling with my family lately, but Tiffiah didn't have shit on Rizzo. Tiffiah wouldn't cook for a nigga without me asking, nor was she the perfect mother she tries to be. That head and pussy were keeping a nigga floating, amongst other things. I had to sniff a few lines just to sit in the house and play husband of the year with Tiffiah's ass. The kids weren't that bad, and little Nadia was getting closer to me. I had been here for days and had yet to see her punk ass daddy. The shit was crazy because she was a smart and beautiful little kid.

"Daddy, Nadia wants apples," Armon came over and voiced while I was watching the game.

Armon was the best big brother, but I saw how he had been doing a few things his fucking momma was supposed to do.

"I got her, little man. Go back to your room, iight."

Armon rushed off, and I went to cut up Nadia apples when Tiffiah walked in, pissed off. Tiffiah had just dropped them off with an attitude, and now she was back with one. I wasn't letting her ass fuck up my high, and I wanted some pussy, so she needed to erase the smug look and come hop on daddy's dick.

"What the fuck is wrong with you?" I asked, and Tiffiah whipped her neck into my direction.

"What did I tell your hardheaded ass about coming at me like that, Croy? I am not your child. I am the mother of your child. The fuck, weak ass nigga." Tiffiah rolled her eyes and went to take her heels off.

I had enough of her shit. Over the last few weeks, I hadn't touched her ass off the strength of the kids always being in her fucking space. Tiffiah's mouth had become ruthless, and I was done ignoring the obvious.

Walking up to her calmly, I slapped fire from Tiffiah face, and she grabbed the same side with tears coming. Something went off in me, and I kept going. I was fucking Tiffiah up, and her cries meant nothing to me.

"Daddy!" Armon yelled.

"Go to your room, Armon!" I yelled, and I grabbed Tiffiah up while she fought against me. I dragged Tiffiah to our bedroom and threw her to the ground.

"Croy, you fucked up. You need to chill, baby. I am so sorry for coming at you like that." Tiffiah cried, and I didn't give a fuck about any of it.

"Man shut the fuck up and swallow this dick." I locked the door, and Tiffiah got on her knees in front of me.

I pulled her hair back and dropped my dick down in her throat. I didn't worry about Tiffiah biting me or no shit like that. She knew if she fucked me over, she was a done deal out here. No nigga would give her ass the life I had. She was stuck with a nigga.

Tiffiah wasn't trying to suck my dick like she used to, so I gripped her head tighter and forced my dick down her throat. Tiffiah was choking, but her mouth was so wet and tight. I couldn't stop myself as I sped up and looked down at her. I knew she was alive, but her eyes were teary and red. I felt my nut coming, and I kept going, but just before I came, I pulled out and let loose on her face. I threw Tiffiah back, and she wiped her face.

"Get on the bed, I ain't done," I ordered, and Tiffiah looked like she wanted to protest but went against it. Tiffiah laid on her back, and I roughly turned her over.

"Croy, please don't—"

Her words were cut short from my dick jolting inside her tight ass. I pull out after a few strokes and spit on my dick before re-entering her tight ass. Tiffiah screams ceased as I fucked her in the ass for what felt like hours. I knew I had ripped her a new asshole, but she was now wet as fuck. The feeling of my dick easing in and out of her was giving me another high, and the coke had my dick hard as fuck. I flipped Tiffiah over, and she was passed out. I still slid in her pussy and fucked her until I came deep inside her.

SLAP!

"What the fuck?" Tiffiah jumped up and tried to scoot to the top of the bed, but she was still in pain.

"Let that be a clear memory for the next time you think about running those gums at me. Go clean yourself up." I mugged Tiffiah as she weakly got up from the bed and slowly went to shower.

I went to join her and made her suck my dick once more for the road. Orion had called a meeting, and I wasn't feeling the need to be there, but my pops thought I needed to, and I knew better than to go against his word.

My father, Farooq, favored Orion so much that I had a little pull when it came to him. My mother saw it and tried to be on my side sometimes, but that was rare. My father was grooming a child that wasn't even his to run his empire and to be honest, I have grown tired of watching in the shadows. I was tired of being treated like I was the stepchild, and Orion was the golden son. Orion wasn't putting in half the work like me, and here he was about to have the whole game.

Today I would be announcing my own team, and if Orion felt like I was coming for him, then he might want to make some new moves. I just needed him to take care of this beef for me so that I could move in the streets with ease. After the meeting, I was holding one of my own, and it was to tear down Orion and my father's empire.

14

Orion

I looked around the table and noticed Croy was here and on time today as I stood at the head of the table. Each crew on our payroll had their right hand standing behind them except Croy. I gave Croy a head nod, and he rose to his feet. The entire room gave him the floor except for Terrance, one of the crew leaders who fucked with the east side niggas heavy.

"Terrance! You have an issue with giving my brother the floor?" I ask, and Croy looked his way. I wasn't for the disrespect, and when Truth noticed my agitation, he walked over to Terrance.

"I mean, Bossman, we are in this mess because of your brother. Why the fuck is he even having a say in how we handle the issue he brought to our tables. I planned on eating, but I guess we are shoving the plate to his snake ass," Terrance said, and Croy moved his way, but Terrance right hand Marco stepped in. Croy eyed him, and Marco looked down at Croy. Marco was a big ass nigga, and there was no way my brother could match him, but it didn't mean Croy would back down.

"Nigga, you don't get to ask questions. If you don't like how I run shit this way, then excuse yourself but leave my walkout money right here for you and your whole crew."

I sat back, and Terrance shook his head before looking Croy's way.

"Take the floor, G," Terrance said, and a slick grin eased over Croy's face.

I noted what just went down and to speak to Terrance when the meeting was over, while Croy told them the plans of our enemies. To see the looks on their faces was price-less, except for Terrance.

"So, we going in strong, right? I fuck with them niggas, but nobody comes before my bread." Terrance said, and everyone agreed.

"I figured you would be the one against it," I said, surprised.

"Nah, your money is still platinum and green, right?" he asked, and I chuckled and nodded. "Then I'm loyal to my crew. No matter what the issue, if my money's right, and your money's right, we straight and I'm riding for y'all. The east side niggas ain't bringing in no money."

I nodded and got back to business.

⸺

ONCE THE MEETING WAS OVER, Croy dipped off, but Terrance stayed behind and pulled me aside. I knew it was to adjust the way he tried to handle Croy, but I needed more from him. Terrance knew more about this beef, and if anyone could be trusted to tell me what went down, it would be Terrance.

"What's up, T?" I asked, sitting down at my desk.

"I just wanted to chop it up before I got back to this money. Check it, Croy is on some other shit. O, he's trying to start his own crew to go against you." Terrance looked like he really didn't want to give me the information, but he didn't want shit to go left either.

"That's a huge accusation, my nigga. Do you have any proof to back that shit up?" I asked, and Marco walked over with the voice memo.

"Hell nah, fuck Orion pretty ass. Once our crew is heavy enough, we are taking his ass out too. We just need to get through this meeting and let them kill off them east side and west side niggas so that we don't have to start business off in the middle of a war."

The recording of Croy speaking to Terrance and Marco on the phone fucked my head up. I knew Croy was in his feelings, but to plan to fuck with me on some sneak shit, and trying to put on niggas that I groomed. Yeah, Croy was losing his mind if he thought I would go down easy.

"How many niggas agreed?" I asked, and Terrance ran down a whole list, just as Truth walked in, looking confused.

Once I was done with Terrance and Marco, I sent them on their way, but to tell Croy they wanted in after the way the meeting went.

"Bossman, we ten steps ahead of you already. Marco told Croy we were down, and Croy told us to pull that shit earlier to make it seem like me and him beefing hard so that nothing looked fishy. I'll have that intel for when he is coming for you if I don't pop that nigga first."

Terrance and Marco dapped Truth and me up and walked out of the Office. Truth sat down across from me, and I ran everything back down for him.

"That nigga's doughnut light is broke." Truth busted out laughing, and I did too.

"What the fuck that mean, nigga? You come up with

the craziest metaphors," I joked while looking down at my phone.

"Croy's hot light's broke. The nigga doesn't know right from wrong, or if he wants to be loyal or a snake. Ain't no way you two are brothers." Truth shook his head.

"That's Farooq's son. Shit, even that doesn't make sense to me." I laughed.

Croy had already started texting me about his wife throwing his shit out, so if I needed him, then he needed some time to handle that. I never called Croy to handle street business anymore after this beef was fueled.

Truth was right, Croy didn't know how to make his moves stick and mean for something, all the while making a positive impact for his team. If Croy wanted my spot, there was more he had to do outside or take niggas from my crew. After this whole beef shit, Croy would have to prove his loyalty to his team the same way I did and gain niggas trust. If not, Croy will leave a whole team to starve, just to make sure he eats, and that team will turn on him in the same amount of time.

"Man, let me get out of here. I must go and check on my sister. I know I fucked up laying hands on her, but I felt like I was losing her too, brah."

I understood that when everything went down the other night. Truth had huge abandonment issues, but this was the first time I heard him admit it.

"I feel you, brah. You need to reach out to your girl too. I hate to say it, but with Tamiko, you were grounded, and you could think and ration with the best of niggas. Right now, you sloppy, and the Truth I grew up with would never be out here looking like that, even before the big money."

"I know a nigga is going out bad. I just didn't see Lola and JB. That nigga could have been told me he was smashing my sister but decided to keep it to himself. That nigga is moving shady, and we need to find a new supplier, I can't keep rocking with him," Truth said, and I nodded.

I had heard about this plug named Amir out in Charlotte, but recently I heard he got jammed up in some shit. I was on the same page with Truth. JB and Lola fucking around was bad for business, and the way JB handled it was fucked up too. At the same time, Truth knows damn well it ain't his fucking business, sister or not.

"Let Lola do her, brah. She knows you got her, and you always will. As far as a new supplier, I was thinking about reaching out to Bleek and Trez out in the Queen City and see what they are talking about. I'll set some shit up and send you the location pin. If it ain't business, it ain't worth the stress. Lola is smart, and she can handle herself. Get my nigga back on his shit and go say sorry to your sister." I pointed my finger like my mother did to us when we were kids, and Truth chuckled.

We chopped it up a little more before I headed out, and Truth made his way to check on Lola. My mother, Marissa, called and asked if I could bring something to keep the kids out of her garden, something Farooq could have done, but he was out of town on business. I called the same fencing company I used for my garden and made my way over. It had been a minute since I saw my nephew, Armon. I missed my little nigga. Since it had been a while, I stopped by Friendly Shopping Centre to get him some new gear and a few games for his PS4.

You could tell it was a hot girl summer out here. It was ass cheeks playing peek-a-boo everywhere. It was even a few MILFs that were stacked like IHOP free Pancake Day. I was only planning to hit maybe five stores, but when I walked into Carter's, I knew I was tripping. Standing in an all-white jumper suit, Rizzo had her big curls swinging and a little shorty on her side. I walked over to surprise her, but her little shorty snitched on me, making me laugh.

"What's wrong, Tamia? Oh!" Rizzo turned and looked up at me. I could see her face flush before she turned away to calm herself.

"Mommy? You okay?"

Little momma was giving me the hardest mean mug while she rubbed her momma's back. Rizzo assured her she was okay and told her I was a nice man who helped her out the other day.

"Oh, well, hello, Mister." Tamia held her hand out, and I took it in mine and squatted to her level.

"Mr. O and I am just fine, how are you?" I asked, and she blushed.

"Fine, you can talk to mommy, but keep her busy while I find my new school clothes." Tamia winked and whispered the last part as best as she could, but looking up at Rizzo, I knew she heard her. Tamia ran off to find her some clothes while I tried again with Ms. Rizzo.

"We meet again," I voiced, and she rolled her eyes.

"You can cut the bullshit. Who are you here shopping for?" she asked, but more so to see if I had kids or not. I knew the tone by now.

"My nephew, I don't have any kids of my own right now. Your daughter is gorgeous, but she's sneaky as hell." I laughed, and Rizzo joined in and looked in her daughter's direction.

"Yeah, watch her come over here with bows, shoes, and pocketbooks in her arms, and not one item of clothing," she joked, and sure enough, that's what I saw her picking up.

"I don't want to hold you, but I wanted to ask the other night, but it seemed like the wrong time. How would you like to go to dinner with me tonight?" I asked, going out on a limb.

Rizzo smiled and looked down at her feet, but I used two fingers to lift her head back to where she was looking into my eyes. Rizzo had me mesmerized with those eyes, and when she licked her lips, my fucking heart jumped, not to mention her deep dimples on both sides of her face. Rizzo didn't have any makeup on, and I wasn't against it, but she really didn't need it.

"If I can find a sitter, then I am down. Take my number down and call me later." Rizzo pulled her pocketbook to her side and fumbled inside, looking for pen and paper.

"You could just put it in my phone instead of fighting your big ass suitcase over there," I joked, but from the way Rizzo looked up at me like I wasn't shit for the comment, I backed off.

Rizzo ran her number off, and I saved it as Tamia walked over with everything Rizzo said she would.

"How about this, momma?" she asked.

Rizzo politely put everything back, and we said our goodbyes. Tamia looked hurt behind her not getting her shit, so while I shopped for Armon, I grabbed her a few things too. What can I say, Uncle O, love the kids.

15

Tamiko

I grabbed my iPad and my purse, hoping my keys were inside so that I didn't have to run back into the house for them. I walked out the door. I was so deep into my purse looking for my keys that I didn't notice Truth sitting on the roof of my car. Just when I had grabbed my keys, I dropped them terrified. It was dark outside, and I was just walking over to Rizzo's house to watch Tamia.

"Oh shit, Truth, you scared the fuck out of me. Get the fuck off my car like that, nigga," I fussed, picking my keys up and locking the house.

My mother Kenya worked the graveyard shift, and since Rizzo had Wi-Fi, I chose to watch Tamia over there so I could get some work done. I was working on a wig line, but I hadn't come up with a dope name for my business. I know everyone was on the weave and wig wave, but it was up to me to be different and give them service that only I can give. I had to own my talent.

"Where the fuck are you going with all that shit? You trying to fuck on another nigga and get laid out, huh?"

Truth walked up on me so quick that I could smell the weed on his breath.

"Boy bye, the only hoe out here is you with your high ass. MOVE! I have to get up there to Rizzo's house to watch Tamia since your homeboy obviously knows how to go after what he wants."

I moved Truth out of my path and hit the lock on my car before walking around back to Rizzo's house. She stayed right behind me, but an old, torn down park area divided us.

"I'm here, ain't I? You think I do this for every bitch I fuck?" Truth asked, and I whipped around to check his ass quick.

"Truth, there is no bitch present, so chill with the loose word. I mean damn, you act like a bitch must drop everything and come running for you when your dick gets hard. I must work to make a living. There is nothing else to it. If ole girl gives you more, then stick to that Omar looking hoe!"

I hurried my ass up the walkway because I was not supposed to be wasting this much energy on Truth. He chose what he wanted and how he wanted to play this game. Now he was butt hurt because I was playing his game better than him.

"Fuck you then, Tamiko!" Truth yelled to my back, and that shit crushed me.

I never thought he would do me dirty, but it is what it is. I had spent days trying to make myself forget Truth, but I wanted to remember every minute of this. I wanted to learn from this, so when the next man tries to break me down or use me, I can be stronger. Using my key, I walked into Rizzo's house just as Truth sped out the back parking lot.

"Hey, you okay?" Rizzo asked, and I nodded. I hurried

and put my things down just as Tamia yelled that she was out of the tub.

"I can grease myself, mommy!" she yelled downstairs, and Rizzo rolled her eyes. Tamia was growing more and more, and not just physically, mentally, and emotionally. Tamia had grown and shown it daily.

Rizzo came back to the living room, and that's when I noticed how fly my girl was. Rizzo had on a see-through white blouse with a white strapless bra, tucked in some light high-waist jeans. She paired them with some white strapped pumps that I needed to borrow.

"Damn bitch, Orion has you coming out like that?" I asked.

When Rizzo told me Orion asked her out, I hurried to offer my services. Anything to get her ass from Croy and his weak ass hustle. Croy was more of a headache when he fucked with your friendship and relationship. There I go again, thinking about Truth's hoe ass.

"Girl, I hope this fit for where ever he has in mind for tonight. I don't even think I should be going."

"Why the hell not? You never go out unless it's with Lola and me. You deserved to be wined and dined."

Rizzo never took time for herself. I hoped Orion knocked the dust right off her pussy.

"I just met this man, and I don't know girl, I'm nervous. I haven't been with anyone since Croy's ass, but already Orion is showing me that he is different, something to look forward to. Ugh, Tamiko, just help me take these rollers down. I need to roll and get my mind right."

Rizzo went to get a chair from her kitchen and her weed bag. I let her roll before I jumped in to start on her hair.

Letting her luscious curls fall, I smiled, satisfied at the outcome. Rizzo looked like a thirty's singer. She just needed a gown and old school mic. Rizzo had sparked the blunt and put it in rotation when there was a knock at the door. I went to answer with the blunt in my hand and there stood Orion and Truth. I rolled my eyes because that nigga was just on some fuck me type behavior.

"What you want Truth, you are crashing their date too?" I asked, and he mean mugged me.

"Move the fuck around, Tamiko. I came to watch my niece too and bring her some shit."

Truth moved past me, bumping me in the process, so I mushed him in the head.

"Y'all in here with the devil's lettuce and shit while my baby up there. Aye boo-boo, Uncle Tru's here!" Truth yelled up the stairs, and you could hear Tamia little feet on the way.

"Hey, Orion, you ready?" Rizzo asked, and from the way Orion looked over Rizzo, I was glad I brought my overnight clothes. Tamia hugged her mother before rushing Truth for all the gifts and bags he brought in with him.

"Yeah, it seems like these two have it under control. You look beautiful." Orion kissed Rizzo cheek, and she smiled.

"Aht aht, have her home by twelve, niggas," I joked as I closed the door behind them.

I looked over at Rizzo's couch, and Truth was showing Tamia a bunch of clothes, shoes, and purses. Since she already had dinner, I let them chill and watch movies in her room while I did some work in Rizzo's guest/play-room. When she first moved in, they didn't have any more two-bedroom units, so they gave her three-bedroom.

"Tamiko, I need to speak with you." Truth startled me, and I looked at the time and knew Tamia had finally tapped out on his ass.

"Nah, fuck me, right?" I asked, and Truth licked his lips.

"Bet," Truth said and walked over to me, flipping my body over and pulling my tights from my body. For all it took for me to squeeze all this ass in those tights, Truth had them off in seconds. Truth lifted my legs, letting them fall into the crease of his arms as he went face-first into my pussy. Slowly teasing my clit, Truth slurped on my pearl, making me moan out in pleasure.

"Daddy's sorry," Truth spoke as he ate my pussy with such passion.

Slowly circling my clitoris, Truth started to suck my clit gently, sending electric shocks all over my body. I could feel my nipples harder, threatening to rip holes through my shirt. I ease my shirt up and play with my nipples while gyrating my hips in Truth's face.

"I need you, bae." Truth said and gripped my ass with the tips of his fingers.

"I need you toooo," I cooed. Fuck, why was he doing this to me right now? There was nothing I could do.

"I need to feel you, ma. Let daddy get his taste so I can feel you. Cum for daddy." Truth said and sped up, sucking my clit harder. I grabbed his head and pushed it further into my pussy.

"Please don't stop, daddy!" I moaned louder.

"Not until you wet this face up. Cum for me, Tam," Truth groaned. I felt his fingers enter my pussy and fuck me before he took them out and eased one in my asshole.

"Fuuuck!" I moaned louder as I felt my orgasm rising.

My body began to shake, and I had to close my eyes, and I came hard, squirting all over Truth's face and shirt. I continued to shake as Truth continued to suck on my clit. It was as if he was controlling my convulsions with each suction.

"Damn bae." Truth smiled and stood to his feet, removing his shirt and unzipping his pants.

I watched as Truth stroked his big dick, and my mouth watered. I sat up and took him in my mouth and swallowed him whole. When we first got together, I could never take all of Truth in one session, but now this was my dick, and I knew just how to please it.

"Fuck suck that shit, ma. Take all this dick down that throat," I moaned each time I saw his dick disappear into my mouth, making Truth shudder. I giggle, and he shakes some more.

"Shit, chill before I cum early. Got damn, Tamiko." Truth watched me, and I locked eyes with him.

I opened wide with my head held high and let Truth hold my head while he fucked my mouth as if it was my pussy. I never knew this shit could really be done, but once I learned, I had Truth going crazy. I could feel Truth's dick jumping and getting bigger in my mouth. I moaned with his strokes as I felt his warm nut easing down my throat.

"Shiiiiiiiiiit!" Truth moaned. I sucked up every drop, keeping my eyes locked on Truth. Truth pulled his dick out and sat down on the foot of the bed. I straddled his dick and eased down.

"Tamiko, I can't do this shit without you. I know I fucked up and keep fucking up, but you keep me solid in these streets. With so much disloyalty and snakes, I never know who I can trust. I know I have a solid one with you, and you have never shown me otherwise. I am sorry I hurt you, and I will never hurt you again, I love you, Tamiko," Truth groaned in my ear, holding my body to his while stroking my pussy from beneath me. Tears slid down my chocolate cheeks, onto his shoulder, and Truth wiped them away before speeding up a little.

"Tell me you love me, Tamiko." Truth groaned, and I

opened my mouth, but nothing would come out. Faster, Truth started to fuck me so hard I was cumming all over his dick in seconds.

"I love you too, Truth!" I screamed as I reached my second orgasm of the night. Truth kept going until he came right after me, but I was so spent I fell into his chest.

I had so much going through my mind, but mostly what Truth had just said. I know he had been smoking and drinking, but I could feel his words were real. If Truth could learn to respect me completely, then we could have something special, but I wasn't sticking around to be played with again. I felt myself drifting off with Truth, but I had to make sure he knew I meant what I said.

"I love you Truth, but I will kill you if you play with me again."

The look in his eyes when he read mine assured me that he heard me. Truth placed my head back on his chest as we both drifted off to sleep. I will make him order Rizzo guest bedroom a new bed in the morning.

16

Rizzo

I was on cloud nine rapping *The Marathon Continues* by Nipsey Hussle. It was my shit, and Orion was on the same wave as me. I wasn't into trap music, but I wouldn't define Nips music to be trap. I felt I was given a few lessons and eye-openers when I vibe with Nip, I can just sit back and focus on what's at hand, but this here made me want to celebrate life.

Orion was taking me to a bar after tiring my ass out at Celebration Station. I was far from dressed for a playground like this, but I didn't give a fuck, and Orion loved it. When he asked if I wanted to race, I was hype as hell. When I brought Tamia's little scary ass, I had to take my time, and these mini cars were made to go fast. I beat Orion in everything, and he swears he let me, but I knew better.

"Aye, I just thought about it, shorty did mug you when we got off the ride." Orion had turned the volume down and passed a blunt that he had just rolled. I wasn't trying to be geeked, but from the smell of the weed, I had to bless these lungs.

"I told you that bitch wanted your ass and didn't think I matched your fly. Ole hating ass hoe." I rolled my eyes laughing and then took a pull from the blunt.

Orion might have been very neat, but he rolled like a hood nigga. That shit was ugly as fuck, and I loved a pearled blunt. My face screwed up as I looked over Orion rolling skills, and it must have shown.

"You talk shit about my blunt, and I'm leaving you on the side of the highway," he smirked, and I covered my sly smile. I just wanted to bite that bottom lip, while running my fingers through his beard.

"I just like a nice pearled blunt, that's all. I can teach you one day," I winked, and he smiled back.

I peeped Orion fixing himself. It took him a few tries, and it made me giggle.

"What's funny?" he asked, and I battled myself on how I should respond. Usually, I would cover it up, but I wanted to go out on a limb with Orion, it just felt right to be honest with him.

"Watching you adjust your mans down there, he must want to play." I smiled, and Orion shook his head.

"Since I laid eyes on you, but I have him on lock, don't worry."

"You should let him." I looked deep into Orion's eyes, and we almost ran right into the truck in front of us.

"You need to chill. Fucking with me, and we won't make it to the bar. I'm not with the games ma, and if you need some dick, I'll get you right." Orion was being more forward than I thought he would be, but it was turning me on.

"Let's go," I said, and Orion sped up, switching lanes like we weren't in this big ass truck of his.

I held on to the beam above my head, but I was scared for my life. I had to give it to Orion. This man was making his way through the traffic. Getting off on the MLK exit, Orion ended our trip in some upscale housing in Pleasant Garden. It was no one outside, the yards were sculpted and most lined with flowerbeds.

Orion pulled up to the last house at the top of the community, and I noticed how it was spaced out from the others.

"This is where you live?" I asked, and Orion chuckled.

"Nah, I just own the house and keep it furnished for when I need to escape. I still live with my parents, but for my mother, not for me. When I have a family, then I'll move out. I'm in no rush for me though."

Orion got out and walked around, opening my door. Taking his hand, Orion led me to the front door and led me inside. It was dark as Orion led me past everything in the living room and went straight downstairs to his master suite. Turing the lights on, it looked like a hotel room down here.

I wasn't insecure about my body, so when Orion sat on the white-lined bed in front of me, I stripped naked right in front of him. Orion's eyes traveled my body, and I could feel them tickling my nipples. I smirk and swayed my hips to music only I could hear. I close my eyes just as Orion's fingertips grace and graze my breasts. Tracing up to my neck, I felt a slightly rough tug back, and I felt those juicy lips press against mine. My pussy screamed for him to make her his belonging.

"You smell so fucking good, Rizzo." Orion's voice vibrates against my ear and neck, sending chills down my spine. I can't speak.

Orion bites at my neck and then softly sucked at the same spot while rubbing my nipple with one hand. I open my eyes to the sound of something and see the mirror coming down over the head of the bed, giving me a full show of what Orion was doing to me. I was getting wetter as I watched him take my body over with his. Even the feeling of his sweater on my bare back was making me squirm in his big powerful arms.

"Look at me, ma. Don't look away," Orion said into my ear, turning me into a puddle.

Orion pushed me over and grabbed my hair, yanking it up to where our eyes met. Slowly sliding his hands down my spine, I arched my back at the sensation. Finally, Orion finds my soaked pussy and slid two fingers inside. Orion had this beast in his eyes, and it was sending my body into overdrive. I closed my eyes, feeling myself about to cum, but then Orion stops.

"Nah, keep them sexy eyes on me, ma," Orion coached me, and I was following every order.

Orion went back to finger fucking me from behind and bit down on his lip as my pussy began to grip his fingers. I start to shake as my first orgasm takes my body over. Instead of stopping and giving me time to get myself together, Orion disappeared behind me and dug his face into my pussy. The feeling was something I could not explain. Orion had me screaming and begging for him to stop, but I knew like hell I didn't want him to, so when he did, I looked back heaving and confused.

"What?" I asked as Orion licked around his mouth.

"You clean your asshole, right?" he asked, and I giggled and nodded.

"Yeah, but you not about to... Fuuuuuuckkkkkk, Orion!" I closed my eyes and lost everything I was going to say to him.

Orion's tongue invaded my ass, and I started seeing stars. It felt so good I had to throw my ass back into his face. Orion played with my clit as he ate my ass, and before

I could beg for him to slow down, I was cumming again, and like before, Orion didn't miss a drop.

"Keep that ass up. You not KO'd, are you?" Orion joked, rubbing my clit slowly, and my body shook with each stroke. I looked at him through the mirror and needed to feel him.

"Fuck me, please." I weakly begged. Orion smirked and began to undress.

"Go lay down. I want to look at you while I make you mine," Orion ordered, and I moved as best as I could. My legs were worn out, but I needed to feel this man.

Watching him undress, I couldn't wait to run my hands over his sculpted chest and toned back. When Orion removed his boxers and freed his dick, I looked at him like he lost his fucking mind.

"Oh, hell nah! Sorry, but I wrote a check my little pussy can't cash. Orion, what the fuck? What you about to do with that?" I asked, sitting straight up. Orion walked over and sat beside me, laughing with his dick looking right at me.

"If you're really scared, we don't have to. I enjoy watching how sexy you are when you cum. Them three wrinkles on the bridge of your nose and the way your bottom lip quivers, shit, that's enough."

Orion kissed my lips, and I pulled him closer. Nobody had ever taken that much time to notice things about me. Laying on my back, Orion spread my legs and placed the head of his dick in my opening.

"Look, none of that crazy chick shit after this, iight?" Orion said, looking me deep in my eyes. I slap his chest and laugh.

"Same here," I smirked.

"No need, after tonight you and this sweet pussy belong to me. There's no reason to do all that when you know it's yours," Orion said, and I eased up and kissed him passionately as Orion eased into me.

At first, the pressure was killing me, but Orion took his time, and inch by inch made his way to my pleasure spot.

"Yesssss, don't stop, Orion!" I screamed fifteen minutes later as I rode Orion, aiming for my fourth orgasm. Orion groaned as he pinched my nipples and fucked me from underneath.

"Shit, cum with daddy!" Orion moaned, and it was my pleasure. I arched my back and gripped Orion's dick with my pussy muscles and rocked my hips when I got to the base of his dick.

"Fuck!" Orion yelled out and sat up, biting my nipple.

Orion held on to my body and started to fuck me back, sending me into the most exhilarating orgasm had ever experienced. I couldn't do shit but shake and pass out on Orion's shoulder.

WHEN I WOKE UP, it was four in the morning, and Orion was in the bathroom on the phone. I didn't want to listen in on him, but he was kind of loud, so I could hear him telling the caller that he needed it delivered right now. I was confused because I didn't know what the fuck was going on. Chucking it up to it wasn't my business, I got up and went in search for the other bathroom to use. When I got back, Orion was sitting on the edge of the bed looking stressed.

"Hey, you okay? I had to relieve myself, and you were in there already." I asked and leaned on the doorway.

"Yeah, uh, I didn't wear anything tonight, and I think it's best I get you a Plan B." Orion was straight forward, and it was kind of offensive.

"Uh, sure, I guess, is that what's being delivered here tonight?" I asked, and Orion looked like he was pissed.

"Were you listening to my conversation?" he asked, getting up and walking up on me. I pushed Orion out of my space and went for my clothes.

"Nah, tell your builder that the walls are too thin for your secretive ass ways. I will gladly take a Plan B, but I will not be here with you!"

I grabbed what could and put it on. I grabbed my shoes and bag and made my way upstairs. Orion was right on my ass, and when I got to the front door, he pulled me back.

"Look, I ain't mean shit by what I said, I didn't mean to come off harsh, but I don't think I'm ready to be a father," Orion said, and I burst out with a hearty laugh.

"Tuh, well, if this pussy and I belong to you, then guess what? So does Tamia! I already have a child Orion, and I don't have time for fuck buddies, so if you don't see anything coming from this," I used my hands to show him, "then we have nothing else to talk about it. Just so you know, I have the implant in my arm, so I won't get pregnant."

I rolled my eyes and was ready to go. Orion walked up to me and grabbed my arms, but I yanked it back.

"Rizzo, I understood that, but I need to see how she reacts to a nigga before he knows if he is father material. I don't force shit, so as much as I want to be with you if Tamia doesn't like me, then I won't be in your life either way. I would love to be a father, but I know not everyone is meant to be one. I don't want this shit to end like this, but if you want to go based on my actions, then cool. Like I said, I don't force shit." Orion backed up, and I rolled my eyes.

"Yeah, I need to get home." I rolled my eyes, and

Orion nodded before going back to get dressed and take me home.

I wondered the whole ride if I had fucked up giving Orion the pussy, but it didn't matter. The dick was well worth it, and if I never saw him again based on tonight, then that would be just fine in a way. I really had a great night with Orion, but maybe his life didn't have room for Tamia and me.

When I finally arrived home, Orion walked around to open the door and walk me up to my front door.

"Rizzo," Orion softly grabbed my arm, and I turned to simply look at him. I wanted to be upset, and I wanted to carry an attitude, but looking into Orion's eyes, I couldn't.

"I know I fucked up tonight. Tamia is you, and if I want to be with you, then that includes her. I want to see you tomorrow night if you can. I can pay for a sitter, or Tamia can tag alone. I just want to be with you, ma, and I don't want tonight to ruin a good future." Orion took my hands into his, and I looked him in the eyes.

"I'll think about it, but thank you for saying all of that, Orion. I know I am a handful and come with baggage, but I must always think about my child. I want you to sleep on the thought of her full time, and if that is something you can do, then call me." I kissed Orion softly on the lips as he let go of my body, and I entered my house.

I went and showered and checked on Tamia. I checked on Tamiko and found her and Truth laid up knocked. Truth eased his head up and smirked, rubbing Tamiko's ass. I laughed and went to my room where sleep found me swiftly.

17

Croy

I watched as the cleanup crew pulled up to the warehouse. Meanwhile, Orion walked out like he was the fucking man. Tonight, was one of the first nights this nigga held court in the warehouse and only bodied one of the niggas. I hated the way he shined even when he wasn't trying. I had taken out the other three niggas coming for us, but only because I wanted the security of having territory when this was all over. Since Orion was taking the heads of the east and west side out, I could claim that turf and use my time there to build against Orion.

"Nigga, are you done?" I asked, and Orion looked at me smiling, but it slowly disappeared as he looked at me. I turned my body to him because Orion looked like he would charge me at any minute, and he wouldn't catch me slipping.

"Yo, check this shit out, I have tried too hard to make you see that I love you little brother, but you cold as fuck. You a snake out here, Croy, and the only reason you still have your life is off momma and my nephew. You wanted the east and west side? Well, it's yours, but you gotta find you some weight and don't even think to ask your pops, this was his call." Orion mugged me, and I was red as fuck.

"Say, who the fuck is you to be down here like his bitch ass message boy." I laughed, but Orion didn't like that shit.

"Fuck you say?" Orion asked, walking up on me and pulling his slacks up. Orion squared up, and I followed suit.

Truth told everyone to stay back and mind their business, and for once, I agreed with his ass. Orion threw the first punch and knocked me in the nose. I dodge the next blow and hit Orion in the side twice with two quick jabs.

It was as if Orion wasn't feeling shit, I was throwing his way, and I felt a clean right hook to my jaw that sent me to the ground. I was dizzy as fuck and felt like I would be sick. I tried to hold it in, but between the drugs and the fight, I was losing more than one battle already. I lost my previous lunch, and Orion jumped back, talking shit.

"Man, fuck this nigga. The streets will teach him!" he spat and walked around me.

I was to fucked up to chase his big ass, but I had something for him. I was coming for my father too. He was on the same bullshit. How the fuck was he going to let Orion keep his supplier, but I had to search high and low for mine. I was his flesh and blood, not Orion, so the favoritism wasn't understood.

I got up and dusted the dried red dirt off my gear, before making my way to my car. I heard them talking shit while I was walking, but fuck them. After I killed Orion, they would be begging me to put them on for some jobs.

I found myself outside of Rizzo's apartments contemplating how to make her change her mind. I hadn't seen or talked to her as in days, and that wasn't like Rizzo. Since I had to handle this, I had put her on the back burner, but I needed to see her. Something about Rizzo gave me clarity in my life, and when I went long periods without her, I showed out. I noticed the pattern, but nobody else did because I never told my family anything about her. My family still thought Armon was my only son, and even though it was fucked up, I was being selfish about my side family. Tamia was something to brag about, but I had to keep my own shit to myself sometimes.

My phone rang, and I knew it was my mother due to the "Dear Mama" by Tupac ringtone.

"Hey ma, how you are feeling?" I answered, and when she took a deep breath before answering, I knew some shit was up. I figured Orion had told her what went down, and she was checking in. She wouldn't step in, but she would at least make sure she was okay.

"Croy Tamir, if you don't come and get this bitch off my lawn, I will spray her ass down and then let Chico out to tear her ratchet ass up!" my mother went off.

"Give me my fucking kids, Marissa! Stupid old bitch!" I could hear Tiffiah going off, and I prayed she shut the fuck up long enough for me to get there. I looked at Rizzo's door but pulled off to help my mother.

When I got there, Orion had Tiffiah in an arm lock like she was one of these niggas in the streets. I hurried and parked my car and jumped out, running up on his ass. Hitting Orion in the jaw, he let Tiffiah go, and she fell to the ground crying and screaming, being all dramatic. Orion and I tussled in the yard until my father's voice boomed.

"Break that shit up! Stop all this shit for the neighbors to see and get the fuck in the house. You too, Tiffiah!" my father Farooq yelled, and Orion and I followed his directions. Me more so than Orion, but after my father gave him a look, he walked in behind me.

When I walked in, I noticed my mother with an icepack on her face, and I looked over at Tiffiah. Her eye was swollen, and so was her bottom lip. I smirked because she was going to be worse when I was done with her ass.

"I'm not sure what the fuck you two thought when you pulled that shit in my fucking yard, but I want someone to speak on it." My father looked between Orion and me, and I mugged Orion with the same in return.

"I pulled up to this nigga manhandling my son's mother like she some bitch off the streets!" I yelled, and Orion waved me off.

"Well, your child's mother was putting her hands on your mother, and that was all I could do to stop her without punching her in her face. You might want to respect your parents' home, youngin'!" Orion was calm now, and that shit pissed me off.

"Fuck all that! Momma's good and can handle herself as you can see."

"Croy, I am right here nigga!" Tiffiah jumped up.

"Sit the fuck down before I end your life here. You touched my fucking wife after she has given her time to tend to your children, one of which does not even belong to this bloodline. I think it's in your best interest that you remain silent while we handle this. You are only family by marriage. Stay in your place Tiffiah, and that is your final warning." My father towered Tiffiah, and she quickly found her seat.

I didn't like how my father was in her face either, but I knew better than to express it.

"Just keep your hands off what's mine, and we will be fine. Tiffiah, get my son and come on," I said, standing to my feet. My father looked me up and down like I had lost my mind, and maybe I had. I was tired of taking their shit, and as much as Tiffiah had caused, I still didn't like how they were coming at us.

"This is your choice, Croy! Now this family loves you

and has always been there for you. Every time something doesn't go your way, you are ready to walk away from us. You owe me more than that if no one else in this room. Now out of respect, I want an apology for the disrespect brought to my doorstep," my mother said, looking at Tiffiah and me. Tiffiah smirked and walked right out the door, and I could see the anger in everyone's face.

"Y'all don't have to worry about me anymore. For years I watched as you both groomed the favorite son, and I accepted what love you wanted to give. I have done so much more for this family than any of you know, and when I'm gone, I hope your golden son can pick up the slack." I shrugged and made my way out of the door.

I could hear them yelling shit to my back, but I kept going. I got in the car with Tiffiah and pulled off.

"Thank you for finally having my back," Tiffiah said, and I looked in the rearview mirror and saw Armon was dead in my mouth. I just nodded my head and hurried to our house.

The drive was about twenty minutes, and Armon rushed into the house. I had just paid a landscaper to fix up my yard, and it looked like that nigga worked off each penny. Tiffiah walked in with the same attitude we had left at my parent's house. When I got inside, I made Armon a snack and sent him to his room with it. I went and found Tiffiah on the phone telling her mom she could keep Nadia one more night.

"Orion really got me fucked up putting his hands on me. I should call my brother to fuck his ass up!" Tiffiah yelled as she ended the call with her mother. I sniffed a line and cleaned my nose as I looked over at her.

"Orion will get his. Fuck him. You need to keep your hands off my mother though Tiffiah, that shit was low, and I have all the mind the fuck your ass up behind it."

"Your mother was popping shit about my parenting, and I was tired of taking their shit. I know I lack in certain areas, but instead of always beating a bitch down, why not help me to improve. I swear I am sick of your family and their uppity ways."

Tiffiah had tears streaming down her face, so I reached out for her to come sit on my lap. The coke was kicking in, and I just needed to feel Tiffiah.

"I just want this marriage to work, and I know I have been a handful, but it's not always my fault. I see how they look at me." Tiffiah went on, sitting on my hard dick.

"Fuck them bae, how about you give me another baby?" I bit down on Tiffiah ear, and she let out the sexiest moan I had ever heard.

Tiffiah removed her clothes and fucked me long and hard. I was high as fuck because I came in Tiffiah more than three times before we both were worn out. Before I could close my eyes, I could hear Tiffiah call out my name.

"I think we should set up Orion and take over. With Orion down, your father has no choice but to call you to handle the street work," Tiffiah suggested, and shit didn't sound bad.

For the rest of the night, we planned that shit out before finally drifting off to sleep. Being loyal to Tiffiah might not be that bad after all.

TWO MONTHS Later

It had been two months since the fight with my brother and me being cut off from the family. Tiffiah had really been playing her role and holding a nigga down while doing so. Tiffiah had me set up with a supplier from Vegas named Mad Dog. The fat fucker had a weird appetite, but his money was good and long. I was stacking in cash and had even moved my family to the east side. We lived more so in the country, but a nigga owned his own seven-bedroom house and was dripping in ice. I had just picked up my second Mercedes truck and was waiting to get my pre-ordered Range Rover Sedan.

"Babe, I guess it worked!" Tiffiah rushed in the kitchen with a pregnancy test waving it around.

I could see her pupils were big as fuck, and that assured me she was high as a kite. Tiffiah stated sniffing powder with me after I whipped her ass and tore her ass open. I knew the coke would help her cope with the shit, but it assured me she would never keep my kids. If I went down behind Tiffiah, I would make sure Armon was good.

"Damn, you know you have to quit that shit." I removed the coke from the rim of her nostril and sniffed it quickly up mine, giving my mellow high a slight boost.

"I don't have to, but I will try. Look, I must meet with the wives in an hour, and I want to get a head start. Apparently, Tony's fucking around on Keisha, and she done fucked his shit up again. I have to make these bitches understand they can't move like that with my nigga in charge, bringing the wrong type of attention our way."

Tiffiah moved her long ass weave from her shoulders, and although I knew the outfit was two thousand bands without the shoes, I had to admit, my wife didn't have fashion in her genes.

"Handle your shit, bae. I have to meet up with Rizzo. She wants to talk later today." I went back to making the beanies and weenies for the kids, and I could feel Tiffiah staring a hole into the side of my face.

"Croy, don't fucking play with me! I love you, and we have been good without her or your family. I really think we should bury that bitch with your family for real babe," Tiffiah said, and I thought about it.

"What about my daughter, Tiffiah? You keep leaving her out like I'm supposed to turn my back on her too." I was getting pissed off, but the coke was keeping me together.

"I got Tamia, babe. I am your wife, and that makes her my stepdaughter, so no way could leave her in some foster center. Rizzo, on the other hand, must go. Look, I don't want to argue nor be late, so I love you, and we are celebrating tonight." Tiffiah turned on her heels and walked out the door.

Fuck what she was talking about. Once I got my brother locked up, I was dropping Tiffiah to make Rizzo my queen. I just needed a little more time to get my plan in motion. I texted Rizzo and told her a place and time to meet me before I made the kids' plate and went on with my day, Tiffiah was on some other shit.

18

Lola

"No, what the fuck I'm saying is that this is not what the fuck we been doing JB, and the girls will not be with this shit." I paced back and forth, trying to avoid the dead bodies sprawled all over the floor in the house JB called me over to.

Rizzo, Tamiko, and I had been cleaning houses, apartment units, and a few business centers for JB's cleaning company. I was all legit, and the money was good because, after a month, we had enough to move out and get us a house. Rizzo and Tamia hadn't moved in yet, but Tamiko was moved in and getting on my last nerve. I was over staying up late listening to her whine about my brother Truth.

"Look, money is doubled for this, and they have no choice, iight. Clean this shit up and don't hit my line until it can't be detected, I showed you how now get it done." JB turned and went towards his car while looking in his phone.

"Nigga, fuck you and this job!" I yell at his back and speed walk past him. JB catches me by my hair and pulls me back. I could feel his massive dick poking at me but was pissed, so he was getting no pussy.

"Yo, I ain't ask for all that shit. You ain't going to get into no shit if you do it the way asked. Your mouth has been ruthless lately, and I really think you forgot who the fuck I am."

JB was so smooth and guided my body to his truck. There was no one around, so when he pulled my sweats down and shoved his dick into my pussy, I couldn't fight back. It was lowkey kinky to me because I wasn't stopping if we got caught, I was love struck over JB's dick.

"Fuck, bae!" I moan as JB fucks me silly.

JB lifts my right leg and pounds my pussy faster, and I was getting smacked in the face with my titties with the speed we were going at. I loved this rough raw fucking JB gave me, I would be sore later, but it was worth it.

"You gone clean this shit, Lo?" JB groaned, pinching my nipples.

"Fuck, yessss!" I moan.

"For daddy, right?"

"Yesss daddy, shitttt!" I can't hold it, I feel myself about to cum.

"Nah, don't you cum yet." JB groaned and slowed down, making my nut ease back.

"No, baby, fuck me harder," I moaned, reaching back for his ass to push him harder.

JB smacks my ass hard as fuck and pushes me back down to where I was laying down on his back seat, but standing outside his car while he fucked me. He sped back up, and I could feel his dick growing inside me. My pussy reacted by cumming, and JB followed. I knew JB had cum deep in me, but it was all good. We had been trying, so if it happened, then we both would be happy.

"Damn, Lola. I gotta go change, ma. Handle this for

me now, and when you get home, I will finish what I started." JB kissed my neck and helped me up.

"You two nasty as fuck!" Rizzo yelled, and Tamiko peeked out her eyes, laughing hard as fuck.

I smirked and kissed JB so sloppy that he smacked my ass before he pulled off, agreeing to call me later.

"So, how many rooms are we doing here?" Tamiko asked, and I got straight to it.

"Look, it's one room that has to be done this time y'all. There are four bodies in there, and we must make it look like they never were. I understand if you leave, but I got JB on this, and I am trained to clean this kind of mess," I said all in one breath. Rizzo looked at me, but I couldn't read her expression. Tamiko's expression was clear, and she was pissed.

"Bitch, you are trying to get me fucking killed! If Truth finds out, he will fucking bury my ass and never tell a soul!" Tamiko said, and I rolled my eyes.

"Truth ain't finding out shit because nobody is saying shit." I waved her off and looked back at Rizzo.

"Fuck it, let's go." Rizzo picked her shit up and walked towards the house.

I smiled and went with her, which made Tamiko follow. Tamiko wasn't down, but she wasn't going to let us do this alone.

"Is this what our job consists of?" Rizzo asked at the finish line. I had to black light going over the room with a spray, and I nodded.

"Maybe, when JB needs us to. You don't have to do every job, but it pays double when we must. I think we can be good at this, and we won't get much time if we get caught."

"Bitch, fuck that! I don't want to do time at all!" Tamiko said, and we laughed.

"We won't, but if anything happened, then I would take the fall," I said honestly. I was pushing this for JB, and it wasn't right for them to do any time behind my bullshit.

"Girl bye, after this job, I think we got it. We just need to work on our speed," Rizzo said, and we finished up the house while talking the job over.

We agreed to only take them when we needed to, and I prayed JB understood that. If not, then oh well, I was out. I would find something else to start my boutique up with what had been saving.

Once we were done, I made sure the girls got in their cars safe before I hopped in mine and called JB. When he dropped his pin, and it was our home together, I smiled and pulled off to get me some dick. I rode thinking about how I was going to fuck my way out of a few jobs. JB had us fucked up!

19

Rizzo

I was in love with the candy apple red 2019 Chevy Malibu I had just bought. Tamia loved to brag about our new car, and I was even happier with the huge down payment I was able to make. Everything was going so well in my life, and I finally knew what real happiness felt like. Orion was playing a massive part in it, and when he saw me with Tamia, I was cute as fuck.

It had been a week since Orion, and I fucked, and I told him to call when he was ready. Since I hadn't heard from him, I chucked it up and tried to move on. Orion owned my thoughts, and it took a minute before could go at least an hour without slobbering thinking about his dick.

Tamia ran up to me one day and said someone was at the door. Me, being the cautious parent, fussed Tamia out as I ran downstairs to see Orion standing in my doorway.

"Hey, short stack." He smiled, and my pussy jumped.

"What are you doing here?" Opening the door wider, Orion walked in, and his cologne smelled so fucking good.

"I came to properly meet Ms. Tamia. I know I said I needed some time, but I can't get your crazy ass off my mind. If Tamia is

anything like you, I know I would enjoy being a part of her life. I wanted to know if you two wanted to run to Concord Mills with me for a day trip?" Orion asked, and Tamia jumped up and down, begging me to say yes.

"Go get dressed, and I'll be up there to help you," I told Tamia, and she did just as she was told. "What took you so long?" I asked, and Orion invaded my space, pulling me into a deep and passionate kiss. Orion pulled away and looked me deep in my eyes.

"I don't know, but it won't happen again."

Orion kissed me on the lips, and I went to help Tamia. We went to Concord Mills, and Tamia shopped until she literally dropped. Orion got us a room for the night, and we ended up there a week visiting Carowinds three times.

Since then, Orion and I had been going strong. Today I was going to meet his family, and I was excited but nervous. I had on a mommy and me outfit with Tamia, and it was peach fitted long sleeve sweater dress, but Tamia wasn't fitted. I wore boots with mine, and Tamia had to wear her Chuck Taylors. I was pacing the floor while Tamia giggled.

"You okay, mommy?" Tamia asked, and I nodded.

"Yes, baby, I just need to call your aunties." I grab my phone just as Orion knocks at the door. "Fuck! Baby let's go." I grabbed Tamia's jacket since it was now cold out, and we opened the door for Orion.

"Hey babe, hey homie." Orion held his hand out, and Tamia dapped him up.

"Is your family nice?" Tamia asked, and Orion nodded.

"The best you could ask for." He winked, and Tamia giggled.

"You look beautiful. Let go I want to beat traffic." Orion kissed me on the cheek, and I thanked him as I locked up and rushed to the warmed car.

The whole ride Orion continued the conversation about me moving out of Harriston Homes. I always spoke about it until I was able to. Now it felt like an obligation, and I didn't like the full-on pressure. I hadn't been robbed or fucked with since the first robbery, so I didn't see the need to move. Honestly, I had been looking at Charlotte since Orion took Tamia and I. There was just more there for me than Greensboro.

Orion finally let it go as we pulled up to the massive mansion where lunch was being held.

"Mommy, they have a big ole yard! I could run for years!" Tamia said, and I could see her leaning up to look out the high window. I told her to sit back until Orion came to a stop, and she leaned back, showing sadness.

"I'll give you a grand tour when we get out, okay?" Orion offered, and Tamia agrees, smiling again. Orion squeezed my hand, and I smiled. When he stopped, Orion got out and helped Tamia and me out.

We walked up the door and inside, and the house was beautiful. Greek statues were everywhere, and plants lined the high ceilings. It felt like I was in a hotel looking at the long wrapped around balcony for upstairs.

"Orion, oh, she is beautiful! Hello, Ms. Tamia," Orion's mother walked up to us smiling and looking just like Orion. She didn't look old enough to be his mother but was glad she was sweet.

"Hello, you are as nice as Orion says you are." Tamia smiled and did some twirl I had never seen before, making me giggle.

"Well, thank you, but you are much prettier than he told me and much sweeter. How about you come and help me finish lunch?" Orion's mother asked, and Tamia was hesitant.

"First, what is your name?" Tamia asked, and Orion's mother laughed before answering.

"Marissa, but you and only you can call me Mimi. Go wait for me right there. I have to speak with Orion, okay?" Marissa asked, and Tamia agreed as she went to wait by the corner.

"What's up, ma?" Orion asked, and you could hear the concern.

"Your brother is coming. Your father requested him here. Please just be nice. I really want to have a good luncheon." Marissa cupped Orion's face and rushed off with Tamia to finish lunch.

I touch Orion, and he turns to me, looking pissed off.

"What's wrong?" I asked. Everything seemed to be going nice, but the mention of Orion's brother made him upset.

"Nothing, my brother is just an asshole who I can't touch. Sorry in advance for this nigga's bullshit. His wife isn't much better." I shook my head.

"Baby, I am here with you, nothing can fuck that up. I'll play nice, but I won't take anybody shit, and you know that Orion. Come on," I said and kissed his lips, making him smack my ass.

"Keep on, and you will have a Jr. on the way. Farooq Moore, you must be Rizzo. Nice to meet you." Orion's stepfather gave me a friendly firm handshake, and he seemed hard up, but soft when he needed to be.

"Same to you." I smiled.

"Your mother is done with the meal. When your brother gets here, Maria will bring him in to be seated." Farooq gestured for us to go into the dining room, and we followed.

Marissa had a full spread of soups and salads at one table, a sandwich bar, chicken nuggets and pizza bar, and a small alcohol bar that I was ready to run through. We were all seated when Maria came around, and when I saw Croy Moore hit the corner, my entire heart dropped into the pit of my stomach. I felt so fucking sick, and when our eyes met, I threw up right on the floor in front of me.

"What the fuck?" Croy yelled as Orion scooped me up and carried me to the bathroom to help me clean up.

"You straight?" he asked as I wiped my mouth, and I turned to him with the towel covering my breath.

"Who is he to you?" I asked, and Orion reached in the cabinet, pulled out the travel size mouthwash, and passed it to me.

"That is Croy, my little brother, why?" Orion asked me, and I stepped back from him. I know I heard him wrong. I had to be fucking dreaming. I started to feel hot all over and dizzy.

"Rizzo!" Orion yelled.

"Mommy! Daddy is here with my brother and the mean lady!" Tamia came running into the bathroom, and that was the last thing I heard before I passed out ad everything went black.

THE SOUND of beeping woke me up, and I saw Orion walk over and rub my hair. Tamia was missing, but both Farooq and Marissa were there with worried looks. I looked back up and Orion and tried to remember what happened that caused me to be here. I didn't feel any pain, but something was strapped to me. When I remembered, I looked up at Orion, but he didn't look upset at all.

"Rizzo, did you know Orion was Croy's brother?" Marissa asked, and I shook my head no.

"Croy told me about you guys, but never gave me

names. I wasn't able to meet you, and until you saw Tamia and I saw him, I didn't know Tamia was being hidden." I let the tears fall, and Orion passed me a tissue.

"This change nothing, ma. Fix your face. You gotta relax, Rizzo. You pregnant," Orion said and shook his head. I could tell he was disappointed but didn't want his mother or me to feel it.

"Wait. What? How far along?" I asked.

"Nine weeks actually, so it's still early. Rizzo, I am so sorry we missed out on so much in Tamia's life. If I had known of her, I promise you I would never have left you out there like we did. I must be honest with you, when everything was put out there about you, I had to do my research. Learning about you from the information I have, I know you come from a good family. Rose is a dear friend of mine, and I see where you get your charm when it comes to Farrow. Farooq used to go out with Farrow back in the day and would always end up locked up with your mother because we both didn't play about our men."

I laughed, and Farooq did too while rubbing Marissa's back. The love he had in his eyes was beautiful.

"All in all, I want you to know that we are stepping up and stepping in to help from here on out, including calling your parents here." She smiled, and I did just that.

Farooq and Marissa gave us some time while they waited for Momma Rose and daddy. Orion rubbed my forehead, but I knew he was feeling some type of way. I remembered how he felt when we first fucked, and he asked me to take a Plan B. I did so, I wasn't sure how I fucked up.

"Penny for your thoughts?" I asked, looking up at Orion.

"Shocked honestly, but I expected it. You have been eating pickles and hot Cheetos with pickle juice as if its cereal. That shit ain't some Rizzo shit." Orion laughed, and I joined him.

"Niggas eat that every day, bae. Don't judge me. How you are feeling about it, though?" I asked, and Orion smiled.

"I wouldn't pick anyone else to share a child with Rizzo. If you are going through with it, I need you to move in with me, ma. I don't like you laying up in the middle of the hood with Tamia as is, so carrying my seed, you need to be under my supervision." Orion gave me a stern look, and I looked away.

"I knew you would use this to make that choice. I was going to tell you I would rather that anyway ugly ass. Where is Tamia, bae?" I asked because I was now getting worried.

"Croy had her. He said you never minded her being with him." My eyes widened and sat straight up.

"What?" Orion asked, pulling out his phone.

"Tamia isn't to be around Tiffiah, his wife. When Tamia was four weeks old, Tiffiah filled her bottle with salt and made her drink it with formula, and I almost lost my baby. I told Croy to keep her away, but I know he doesn't. She hates Tamia, and she will hurt my baby. I have to get the fuck out of here!" I yelled and pulled out my phone to call Lola and Tamiko.

Orion assured me he would find her and made a few calls. Everyone met up at my room right as I was being discharge, and Farooq and Marissa agreed to let us use their house to finish planning. I was worried sick, but I had to listen and get my game face on. Croy was petty, but I planned to get my baby away from that bat shit crazy family!

20

Tamiko

"Truth, we supposed to be on the way to them people's house. Why are we at Popeyes?" I asked because Truth was pissing me off. Last night I caught his ass talking to some bitch on the phone, and he swears it wasn't shit. Truth had been doing so good, but now here he was fucking up again.

"We are just going to get us something to eat now and some chicken to pull up with," Truth said and jumped out, going inside.

I texted Lola to see what was up, and she said JB had just pulled up at the house, and they would wait for us. There was a knock at my window, and when I looked over, I saw the girls from the club and mall together. The girl I hit with a bottle was holding a gun and swung it to break the window. I moved over as glass sprawled into my lap.

"Oh bitch, beat my ass now!" she yelled, and she and her sister pulled me out from the car.

As soon as my feet hit the pavement, I hit the Omar looking twin in the throat, and she grabbed her throat, trying to breathe. Her sister jumped on me and was working me well until I knocked her cockeyed ass in between her eyes, making her fly back.

"Come harder, bitch!" I yelled as I squared up with both these bitches, and by now, everyone was crowded around us.

"Move! Man, get the fuck out the way. Bae! Move the fuck around Leni and Lenox! I told you all bets are off when it came to Tamiko. You don't fuck with this one!" Truth pulled his gun and aimed it at both.

"You foul as fuck Truth, be careful out here," Leni smirked and pulled Lenox, AKA Omar back.

"This ain't even over, bitch!" Lenox spat at my feet, and I laughed. I walked over to Truth, but he was mugging me.

"Look at my fucking car, brah! FUCK!" Truth paced and then jumped in his car.

I had never seen Truth this pissed off, and to be honest, I was scared. I let him cool down while I went to get me something to drink. When I went back outside, this nigga was gone. I called Lola, and she agreed to come and get me. I didn't say a word the entire ride to the Moore's resident, but I was on my bullshit soon as I laid eyes on Truth's ass.

When we got there, I stormed inside and slapped the shit out of Truth, making him stand and mug me all in my face.

"Them bitches started with me, and *they* broke your fucking window, but you leave *me* there alone? Fuck you Truth, and after this is all done, I want you out of my fucking house!" I spat and head butted the fuck out of Truth before Orion grabbed me up and hauled me to another room with Rizzo right on my ass, and Lola behind her. I was pissed, and right now, I needed Truth's bitch ass in the room, not them.

"What the fuck, Tamiko?" Lola asked, closing the door as Truth yells carried throughout the room.

"The fucking twins jumped me at Popeyes earlier and busted that nigga window in the process. I swear I'm going to kill them bitches the next time I lay eyes on them. To top shit off, Truth's hoe ass left me up there because he was pissed off about a damn window."

I threw my hands up and paced the floor.

"I am going to beat his ass for that stupid shit, but right now, we need to focus on getting Tamia from out of Croy and Tiffiah's care. I know that bitch is evil, and I need my niece to be okay before I can handle anything else. Them bitches are as good as buried if you ask me," Lola said, and Rizzo nodded.

"Sorry, Riz, that nigga just pissed me off." I rolled my eyes, and Rizzo got up and hugged me.

"I understand, pooh. Calm down so we can boss up on his ass like we planned. You can talk to him later, okay?" Rizzo smiled and got me a cool rag to wash my face.

Once I was good to go, we walked back into where everyone else was sitting, and I immediately apologized to Farooq and Marissa about my behavior, but they both understood. Everyone talked, and Marissa was able to get Croy on the phone. When he agreed to meet her to talk about their lunch, everyone breathed and hoped that we could find Tamia. Everyone went their own way, but Truth sat there mugging me, and I matched his anger with a mug of my own.

"Fix your fucking face. I didn't mean to leave your ass, but I was upset, and I needed to leave," Truth had the nerve to say. I just giggled at his ass.

"I could have gone to jail, nigga! You left me there alone as if they couldn't have come back and killed me. Fuck you, Truth! The only person you ever think about is yourself, and that shit is clear. You wanted me back because I make YOU better, but not once did you think about your effects on me!" I had a few tears fall, but I quickly wiped them away.

"Selfish? Tamiko, I always think about you and the way my life mixes with yours. I might not handle or move the way you want me to, but fuck, a nigga is trying. I have never had to commit to a female, so yeah, I might fuck up. If you can't hold a nigga down and be there for his growth, then bye! I ain't ever been for keeping a female who doesn't want to be kept," Truth said and stood to his feet.

I nodded my head while I grabbed my things. Lola and JB walked towards the front door, but Lola looked at me like she was worried.

"You good, Tamiko?" Lola asked, looking at Truth like she wanted to kill his ass.

"Yeah. JB, you mind taking me to the house?" I asked and walked their way. JB nodded, and we were out the door. Truth really fucked my head up thinking he meant everything he said months ago. I wasn't even mad with him that his little side bitch jumped me, but I was hurt that he didn't show any type of compassion of how I was feeling, not to mention this nigga left me at the fucking fight scene like them witnesses wouldn't rat me out with the quickness.

When I got home, all I wanted to do was take a shower, but I was so tired from working, and the day I had, so I fell right to sleep.

I WOKE up to banging on my door, and I already knew who it was. Truth had me fucked up if he thought he was about to fuck with me tonight. I jumped up to get the door, but at the same time, my phone rang. I looked back, and the banging continued, but something told me to take the call first. Seeing Truth's name, I rolled my eyes and answered with a big attitude.

"What? You are already banging down my fucking door, WHAT, TRUTH!" I yelled and made my way downstairs.

"Bae, please don't open that fucking door. I am two minutes from the house." Truth sounded out of breath, and at the same time that the words left his mouth, I heard a window bust upstairs. Looking that way, I saw flickering lights coming from the room I had just left. Now I was scared as fuck.

"BAE!" Truth yelled, and I couldn't say shit. Window after window crashed, and the house was quickly going into flames. I grabbed the gun JB made us keep here was walked out my front door. There before me stood Leni and Lenox, looking like death itself. They both wore white and black face paint, and it was weird, but nothing this gun couldn't stop. These bitches still bled like I did, so I hoped they were ready for whatever. This time they were on my property, and I had all rights to shoot if their bodies fell like they were coming inside.

"You two are some persistent ass hoes. What's wrong, Omar?" I smirked and walked off my porch. The flames would take over the house before I knew it, so I wanted to get further away.

"I told you this wasn't over. I want my fair fight, and after I beat your ass, I'm going to put three hollow tips in your, ma." Lenox squared up with me, while Leni aimed a gold gun at me.

I wasn't scared of nobody, and if today was my time to go, then fuck it, at least I knew what I was up against. Right before Lenox could run up on me, Truth pulled up and jumped out. Leni aimed her gun at him, but she let him walk over to us.

"You two really thought I wouldn't find out about your little plan? You move fast, but I am always to steps ahead." Truth said, and Orion and JB walked up with their guns on Leni and Lenox. The twins looked defeated but pissed off. "Get these bitches out of here. We will handle them in a few," Truth said and turned to me. I passed him the gun and then stopped Orion and JB.

"Nah, Lenox feels like she was cheated in the past. JB, let sis go so I can finally give her some fair licks and end this question of who beat who."

I walked up a little to give Lenox the same space. I knew I cheated when I hit her with the bottle, so here was her fair fight, but it would be her last. Truth grabbed my arm and looked at me to confirm I was sure, and I nodded, taking my arm back. It still wasn't fucking with him.

"Please let me go so I can drag this burnt black roach!" Lenox yelled.

"Truth, you sure you want that. You know both of our hands registered in these streets." Leni yelled and laughed with Lenox. JB let Lenox go, and she wasted no time running up on me.

Lenox thought I was a punk, but when she reached me, I knocked her ass right in the brim of her nose and again in the side of her eye. Lenox fell back, and Leni was trying to escape Orion's grasp.

"Get up, bitch!" I yelled, backing away to give her space.

Lenox got up and ran up again, hitting me in my lip and splitting my shit instantly. I kept swinging, and I was bopping Lenox in her head and face. When blood started to pour from her nose and eye, Lenox began to call out for someone to break us up. My eye was swollen, but I was still going.

"Hell nah, fight me, hoe! You mad about this nigga, right? Fight me, bitch!" I hit Lenox in her jaw, and she let go of my hair and fell back to the ground. I kicked Lenox in the stomach and chest before Truth grabbed me up and moved me away from Lenox.

"Yeah, bitch! So next time you see me, make sure you walk the other way, ugly scar face hoe!" I yelled as JB went to get Lenox up.

"My baby! Truth, you let her kill my baby! You dead, nigga! You were just eating my pussy, and now you are letting some rundown hoe kill out baby?" Lenox yelled, and I stopped dead in my tracks.

I looked at Truth, and he wouldn't even look at me. Truth kept trying to push me towards his car, but I pushed him off me while grabbing my gun. JB saw me and pushed Lenox away from his body while I let my shit off in her ass. I turned to Truth and shot his ass twice in the leg and side. JB rushed me and grabbed the gun from my hand, while Truth laid there motionless. JB threw me in the car, but before he closed the door, I stopped him with tears in my eyes.

"Put both them bitches in the fire they started." I moved over and slammed the door.

I watched Orion put one in Leni's head before they did just as I told them. Orion and JB put Truth in Orion's truck, and Orion sped off. JB got in his car and looked at me through the window, but by now, I was no good. Truth had brought the worse out of me, and it was clear. I didn't regret shit, and as JB drove me to his crib to be with Lola, I thought of my escape plan.

21

Rizzo

I sat at Orion's house and just wanted my baby. I didn't know what she was doing or how she was being treated, and that bothered me. One thing was for certain, Tiffiah hated the ground Tamia walked on, and she was only a kid. Tiffiah wanted Croy all to herself, and if that meant taking out Tamia, then Tiffiah would. There were already rumors that she ran over a kid and paid off some boy to take the charge. I wouldn't put shit past her dumb bitch.

Orion went out saying it was something going on with Tamiko, and I wanted to go, but Orion was dead against it. Since he found out I was pregnant, Orion was extremely cautious around me, and it was bugging me. The doctor said I was doing good, and I wasn't high risk, so Orion needed to chill. When the front door pushed open, and he rushed in with Truth in his arms, I hurried over to help confused about what happened.

"Farooq has a doctor coming, babe. Go to JB crib and check on Tamiko's hot ass. She fucking shot him, yo."

Orion laid Truth down on the couch, and I went to get some towels and rags. Truth didn't look good, and I had everything flowing through my mind now. I didn't know how Lola was reacting to this news because Truth was her heart, and although Tamiko was her best friend, Lola would kill Tamiko about her big brother. My phone rang, and it was Lola herself. I was hesitant to answer, but I did just to make sure she wasn't on her way to jail.

"Lola, please tell me you didn't kill her?" I answered.

"Kill who? What the fuck are you talking about? I called you to tell you that Tamiko and I are on the way to your crib to blow one and talk. Tamiko said she had something heavy to tell me, and bitch, I am worried, so meet us there," Lola said.

"Okay, let me tell Orion, and I'm on the way. I need to get Tamia's plush L.O.L doll for WHEN she comes home. I'm on the way." I hung up, and Orion looked at me like I was crazy.

"Where you are going?" Orion asked.

"To my apartment. The girls are there, and I need to make sure Lola doesn't kill Tamiko when she finds out she might have killed her only family," I said, grabbing my jacket and putting my boots back on. Orion gave me this unsure look, but I shook it off.

"I'll call you when I get there and when I am on the way back, I promise." I walked back to him and kissed his lips.

I said a prayer for Truth as the doctor, JB, and Farooq stormed into the house and started to move Truth. I took that as my cue to leave and headed to Harriston Homes one more time.

———

WHEN I GOT THERE, Lola and Tamiko were already smoking, but Tamiko was distant. Lola looked worried as fuck, and she had every reason to be. Looking at Tamiko, I wondered what pushed her so much that she felt the need to end the man's life. No dick was that serious, but thinking about Orion, maybe it was. I would make the city bleed behind Orion Semaj Lahey.

"Hey Rizzo, look at this bitch! I swear if Truth doesn't pick up and explain her fucking face, I am going to fuck his next car!" Lola rambled, oblivious of what was going on.

When I dropped my bag and didn't say anything, Lola studied my face, and Tamiko started to cry as she looked at me as well. Tamiko knew I was informed about what she had done.

"What the fuck? Am I missing something?" Lola asked, getting frustrated.

"Truth isn't going to pick up," Tamiko voiced as tears fell from her eyes.

I sat beside Lola as Tamiko ran down everything that happened. I couldn't help but feel like we would never be free of drama. If looks could kill, Tamiko would be dead from the death stare Lola wore. Lola jumped up, and I was right with her worried she would kill Tamiko's ass. Instead, Lola walked towards, and the door, and I went after her.

"Lola, I know you are upset—"

"I need to make sure my brother is okay. This bitch is in her fucking emotions, and now he might be dead. I told you to fucking leave that nigga and his hoe ways alone, but no, a bitch had to run back!" Lola yelled into my house, and Tamiko rushed to the door.

"I said I was sorry, Lola, and I understand you fucking upset, but you are not about to disrespect me like you wouldn't have done the same," Tamiko said, and Lola looked like she wanted to say something but decided not to.

"For your sake, you better hope my brother is good!"

Lola turned and sped off in her car to check on Truth. Tamiko backed into the house and slumped on the couch. I went to join her to see where her head was at while I texted Orion to let him know I was good.

"Why did you have to shoot him, Tamiko?" I asked, and she shook her head.

"When that bitch yelled pregnant, I lost my shit, Rizzo. I love Truth more than I have ever loved any guy I ever fucked with. Truth had turned me into this savage little by little with his shit, and I was tired of just taking his shit. Sure, you both warned me about Truth, but by then it was too late. I have been head over hills for this man since we first met. We were in love, but I think I was going harder for him than he was for me. After tonight that is a guarantee," Tamiko cried and covered her face.

"You need to let him go if he pulls through. Truth might kill your ass. To be honest, bitch, I don't know what the fuck you were thinking. I get that you were hurt, but you must deal with this mess you made. Fuck, come on. You can at least see if he pulls through," I said, and Tamiko shook her head.

"Nah, fuck Truth, and if he doesn't make it, then that's on him. I told that nigga to be careful with me. I'm going to my mother's house." Tamiko got up with a nasty attitude, grabbed her shit, and left me there looking stupid.

If she didn't want to go and Truth died, she would hate herself forever, but that would be on her. Instead of heading back to Orion's house, I headed over to my mother and father's house. Right now, I just needed to hear their wisdom.

⸺

"HEY BABY GIRL, it's late, you okay? Did something

change with Tamia?" my daddy answered the door, and I shook my head and fell into his chest, crying my eyes out.

My dad pulled me into the house and sat me down on the couch while he went and made me some water.

"Rizzo, talk to me." My daddy was confused, and I was too, which was why I was here. I ran down everything I could for him as quickly as I could. I tried to be quiet since my mom was asleep, but he got it all.

"Now, Tamiko doesn't want to go and check on Truth, and right now, I don't know where my friendships lie." I shook my head and wiped my eyes and nose with the tissue daddy had for me.

"Rizzo, you are putting so much on you, and you should only have one focus, Tamia. Tamiko and Lola will either work shit out or split up, but family is over everything, and you know that, so if Lola decides to remove Tamiko from her circle, she had every right. You just have to choose what you're going to do is she does cut her off," he said, and that was something I didn't want to have to do. I was hoping they would hash shit out and come together for the family, but I was far off.

"I just didn't think Tamiko had it in her to shoot him, daddy," I said, still trying to imagine how things went down.

"It's always the quiet ones they least expect, trust me," my mother said, scaring us, making her chuckle. "Rizzo, Tamiko was wrong, and if she values her friendship, she will do anything to make it right, but not kiss ass. You shouldn't even expect her to. As a woman, you know how bad love can hurt and how fucked up it makes your mind and psychological decisions. Let her take this time to figure out where she wants to be. Any word on Truth?" my mother asked, and I forgot to even check my phone.

Orion had called me back to back within the last hour,

and I missed each call. I hurried and called back in fear of the worse coming my way.

"Bae, where the fuck you at yo? I know you saw me blowing your shit up!" Orion yelled into the phone, and I looked at the phone as if I dialed the wrong number.

"First off, calm down, Orion, I am at my parents' house. Is everything okay? How is Truth?" I asked, and I heard Orion taking a deep breath, slowly letting it out and then answering.

"Awake and pulling through. He asked for Tamiko soon as he opened his eyes. Lola's here and she's not leaving his side. I need you here, ma. I'm sorry for coming at you like that, but I need you in my sight right now," Orion expressed, and I smiled.

"How about you come and get me, and we go home together?" I asked, and Orion agreed before I hung up.

"Truth is going to make it, and he wants to see Tamiko," I told my parents, and my mother closed her eyes and thanked God for blessing and sparing Truth tonight.

"Are you going to tell her?" my father asked, and I started a text to her then stopped.

"I will let her know that he is awake and asking for her, but it is up to Tamiko to take the step and go to see him. I think they both need to talk and take some time apart, but that's up to them." I said, sending the message.

"How are you feeling?" my father asked, and I shrugged.

"Worried, restless, and worried some more. I know Croy loves that little girl and would never let anything happen to her. At least the old Croy would. The man I have seen lately was on something, and he didn't look good. I just know that trifling ass hoe Tiffiah will bury my baby if given the chance, and here I go in orange writing you two letters." I shook my head and took a sip of the water.

"Tamia will be fine. Tiffiah isn't that crazy, and if she is, then Croy will kill her before we do. I know God is watching over my grandbaby, plus Tamia is stronger than she looks." Momma Rose said, and I smiled.

"Hell yeah, I meet with Farooq tomorrow, so I'll let you woman folk talk. I love you, baby girl." Dad got up and kissed my forehead and then did the same for my mother.

Momma Rose came over to sit beside me and hugged me tightly. We sat there and talked until Orion came, and we headed to his house. Tamiko never texted me back, and when I tried to call, I was blocked. I felt some type of way, but Orion wouldn't let me stay in my feelings for long. After fucking my brains out, I was out like a light thanks to Orion Lahey.

22

Croy

Tamia's spoiled ass had only been with me for a day, and I was ready to ship her ass back to her hoe ass mother. I couldn't believe Rizzo was fucking my own brother and going strong from the way my mother sounded when she invited us to lunch. When she saw me and got sick, I was pissed. Rizzo felt disgusted by me, and her face showed it. When she passed out, and they rushed her off to the hospital, I took that chance to get my baby girl. Tamia was the only person I knew still loved me, and when she didn't cry to leave with me, I figured she was good.

Since we got to this house, Tamia had been begging to go home and wasn't paying Tiffiah any mind. It was as if Tiffiah didn't exist to Tamia. I was sick of Tiffiah fussing at me about Tamia and had given her to go-ahead to discipline Tamia. Tiffiah was my wife, and if Tamia were going to be here, then she would act accordingly.

"Ahhhhh!" Tamia's screams for help could be heard throughout the house, and Armon had to close his door to try to get some peace. I had heard enough myself and got up to end whatever session Tiffiah had started.

"Yo, what the fuck, Tiffiah?" I boomed, snatching Tiffiah off Tamia and swinging her across the room.

I rushed over to my baby, and she was too weak to move any further away from me. Tamia was bruised up and had welts all over her little body. Tiffiah had even ripped some of her skin open, exposing her innocent flesh.

"Your daughter called me an evil step bitch! Yeah, I tore that ass up, the fuck!" Tiffiah jumped up and tried to run up on Tamia, but I stood and knocked her ass back to the ground. Standing over Tiffiah, I picked up and slapped her silly.

"Bitch, you fucking tore her skin open! Don't you even look her fucking way. What the fuck is your issue with Tamia?" I yanked Tiffiah up, and blood leaked from her mouth as she spoke.

"I won't be disrespected in my house!" Tiffiah yelled back, pissing me off even more.

I dragged Tiffiah out of the room and to a spare room in the house. The room didn't have shit in it, and I threw her body in there, locking it from the outside. Tiffiah screamed to be let out of the room, but I had to check on my baby girl.

When I returned to the room where I left Tamia, she was knocked out, and her body was on fire. I started to get paranoid because if she died on my hands, I would never forgive myself. This wasn't the plan, and I was fucking up again. Hitting myself in the head, I tried to think of what I should do.

"Daddy, you okay?" Armon asked with an innocent and worried expression.

"Yeah, go pack some clothes and toys son, we have to leave." Armon ran to his room, and I went after him to help him. Nadia was with Tiffiah's mom, so I knew she could chill there for a while. I packed up everything electronic of Armon's and wrapped Tamia up. Once I had them both in the car, I went back for Tiffiah. Even though I didn't give Orion or my father this new address, I was dumb enough to put everything in my name. Orion worked in realty, and it would be nothing for him to find out where I laid my head. I went back for Tiffiah and dragged her ass out of the house. An older white woman was walking her dog and saw us fighting, but she turned and hurried the other way.

"Where are we going to go, Croy?" Tiffiah asked, and I backhanded her so hard her head flew back and hit the seat.

"Let me fucking think, man!" I yelled. At this point, I was driving like a mad man.

I looked back to see if Tamia woke up yet, but she was still asleep. I made a quick right and headed towards Moses Cone Hospital instead. Tiffiah was against it saying they would ask me questions and possibly take her from me.

I got nervous, and so when I pulled up, I jumped out and gently pulled my daughter's body from the car. Nobody was outside, but the glass showed my every move. I laid my baby girl down on the bench outside and rushed back to my car. Before I got in the car, I noticed a familiar face coming my way. Kenya, Tamiko's mother, was rushing to get to Tamia.

Worried, I peeled out of the parking lot, headed to an apartment I had in Ray Warren. I needed to take these niggas out before they did me in. It was planning and take out time.

23

Lola

I sat here watching as the nurse changed Truth's bandage while Rizzo texted me back. It had been two days, and there were no signs of Croy, Tiffiah, or the kids. Orion even went to Tiffiah's momma house, but she had moved out. When Tamiko's momma found Tamia, I was grateful. Nobody had yet to speak to her except Rizzo, and it was going to stay the same with if it was up to me.

"Why you over there mugging?" Truth asked as the nurse walked out of his room.

Truth was home, and I was here with him to make sure he was okay. Since Truth wouldn't let me stay over, any free time I had I was with him. My brother was my everything, so I needed to keep my eyes on him. Croy had it out for Truth just as much as Orion, and there was no way that I would let Truth get caught lacking.

"Because I still don't understand why your homeboy ain't found Croy's hoe ass. I swear if I lay eyes on that nigga, he is a dead man," I said, and Truth laughed.

"Lola, that nigga Croy is as good as dead you hear me?

Look, have you talked to Tamiko yet?" Truth fixed his mouth to ask me, and I looked at him like he grew three heads.

"Fuck her! Did you forget that she was the one that pulled the trigger? That bitch is the reason you in that fucking bed now!" I yelled, and Truth shook his head.

"Calm all that yelling down. You mad? Okay, we get it. Tamiko shot me out of anger and pain. You don't know the half of what I have put that girl through, so when Lenox told her about being pregnant, she lost all her shit. I would have killed her ass if a nigga even faked like she was carrying his seed, so I ain't pressed, not to mention your girl has a kill shot. She knew what she was doing." Truth said, and I waved him off.

"She knew better than to shoot you period. How would she feel if I shot her momma for coming at me sideways back in the day? Would she be fucking with me then?" I asked pissed off that my brother was taking up for Tamiko.

All my life, I never heard my brother taking the side of a female over me, but that wasn't what hurt me. Tamiko was my best friend, and I knew her before I knew Rizzo, so I felt like she didn't care how shooting Truth would affect me.

"You have to forgive her, Lo. She is your sister more than anything else. I fucked up, and I must own up to that shit. I think you need to go check on her for real," Truth said, and I rolled my eyes while gathering my things.

"Where you are going, man?" Truth sat up the best he could and asked me.

"I'm going to treat myself to lunch. You are obviously high off them meds. I'll be back in an hour." I blew Truth a kiss and walked out to my car.

I needed to get away, but I had nowhere to go that

didn't remind me of what was going on. JB was that place, but he was out of town on some business meeting. I was growing tired of him getting up and leaving me behind, not to mention JB trying to pry me from Truth when he needs me most.

JB was once everything I wanted in a man, but recently, he had been so damn demanding, and I wasn't into being forced to do anything. Part of me thought maybe he had an outside family, but I didn't want to believe that shit. JB was a good man, and every good man had their flaws, so I wasn't tripping. A while ago, I found mail from DC to a woman with his last name, but for all I knew, it could be that man's sister. If it were something for me to see, it would be more forward than a piece of mail. I tried to call him, but like always, he didn't answer. Since he didn't pick up, I made my way on to Cherry's Fish and Chips. The Love Boat combo was calling my name.

I sat down, and soon as I looked up from my menu, I regretted it. Tamiko was eating with her mother, and Kenya noticed me and nodded her head towards me, making Tamiko look up. We shared a look before Tamiko stood and made her way over to me. Tamiko looked bad, and not at all like my best friend, and for a second, I felt for her. Maybe she was hurting about Truth as much as I was but didn't know how to express her feelings.

"Hey, Lola, you have time to talk?" Tamiko asked, leaning on the seat in front of me.

"You have about ten minutes before they bring my lobster, so make it yours." I sat back while she sat down and waited to hear what Tamiko had to say. I prayed she made it good and didn't disrespect my brother while speaking because I was over this nice shit with her.

"I know I fucked up shooting Truth, but I know I hurt

you too. Truth is your everything, and I know I should have thought first, but who does? Lola, now you know I am the first to say think before you react, but when I heard her say she was carrying his baby, I lost it."

"Is that a fucking excuse, Tamiko?" I yelled, and everyone, including Kenya, looked our way. Kenya looked like she wanted to come our way, but Tamiko stopped her.

"No, it's damn sure not! What you don't know is that Truth forced me to abort not one, but two babies two years ago," Tamiko said, and I thought back to when she wouldn't come out and had been depressed. Rizzo and I thought it was just a bad break up or something but never knew that much.

"Truth promised he wouldn't tell you or anyone else for that matter. Then I heard Lenox saying she was pregnant, and I lost everything in my sane mind. There is nothing to excuse what I did, but I needed you to understand. I am so sorry, Lola." Tamiko said, and I got up to hold her. Tamiko cried in my arms, and I felt for her. JB forced me to get an abortion after our first time, so I knew where she was coming from.

"You did hurt me, Tamiko, but I shouldn't have cut you off like that. This past few days have been hard, but if I had you, I know it would have been a little smoother. Truth is an asshole, and I told your ass that, but I'll be damned if he doesn't love your hot ass." I laughed, and Tamiko joined in wiping tears.

"That nigga is lying, He just wants to see me so that he can kill my ass," Tamiko joked.

"You're probably right too!" I laughed. Tamiko hugged me again, but this time tighter, as if she would never see me again.

"I'm going to finish lunch with my moms and then go see my niece. I know Rizzo is probably pissed with me for not replying to her message. I can't believe Croy's ass." Tamiko shook her head.

"Me either girl, but he will get what's coming."

"What you mean? They haven't found him yet?" Tamiko asked, and I shook my head. Tamiko looked like the wheels in her head were turning, but she cut me off before I could ask what was up. "Well, enjoy your lunch, and maybe I will see you at the hospital?" she asked, and I nodded before hugging her.

"I love you, Lola," Tamiko said, and it confused me.

"I love you too, sis." Tamiko let me go and walked back over to enjoy lunch with her mom.

My food came soon after, but I asked for a to-go platter instead. I wanted to get to Truth and make sure he was okay. When I stepped out, I ran right into someone and dropped my plate.

"FUCK!" I yelled.

"Damn, my bad, ma. I'll get you another—"

Dude looked up into my eyes, and I swear he was sexy as fuck. Dude had some crisp Air Force Ones on with a white LA sweater on. His fresh line up went into the trimmed beard. When he smiled at me, I saw pretty white teeth. I had to blink back because he was speaking with his hand out and everything.

"Uh, sorry, you name again?" I asked, shaking his hand.

"Terrance ma, and you?" he asked, getting a little closer.

"Lola, nice to meet you, but I need that plate you started to offer," I said, pointing back at Cherry's.

"I got you, Ms. Lola. Check this. You can wait in my red Benz right there, it warm already." Terrance got a little more in my space, letting his cologne make love to my nostrils. It was something about a good smelling man that turned me on.

"Nah, I'll wait in my own royal blue Benz, but thank you." I winked and walked right to my car while he watched. I saw him walk into Cherry's and texted Rizzo as soon as he disappeared.

Me: *Biiiiiitch!*

Lil Sis1: *Girl, what and who?*

Me: *I just met a fucking gawd coming out of Cherry's. I have so much tea coming your way.*

Lil Sis1: *Well, don't get me caught up in you and JB mess. But fuck the gawd and see if he worth the bullet to the head. Bye!*

I sat there dying laughing in my car as I texted Rizzo. I told her that I spoke to Tamiko and that she would be there to see Tamia after her lunch with her mom. Rizzo was happier than I expected, but before I could respond, Terrance was walking out with my plate.

"Thank you, and you got it all right." I smiled as I inspected my plate.

"No problem, ma. You have a good day." Terrance pulled out of my window, and I watched him stroll to his car from my rearview mirror. Sure, enough, he jumped in his red Benz and peeled off into traffic.

I looked at my plate again before I pulled off and noticed a piece of paper hanging out. I had to laugh at the fact that he placed his number under my damn lobster. I grab my phone and text his number.

Me: *I almost lost three digits in the butter sauce.*

336-555-8976: *But you got lucky. Don't lose it.*

I smiled as I pulled off and headed back to Truth. I knew I told Rizzo I would be up there, but I needed to eat, and Tamia couldn't be around seafood due to her allergies. Terrance was cute as fuck, but I knew I couldn't go there with him. Rizzo was right. JB would kill Truth and me after Truth tries to kill him. I just wished JB was giving me the attention Terrance just did. I wanted JB to look at me the same way. I shook Terrance off and charged it to the game, just as JB texted and said he would be gone longer. *This is fucking bullshit!*

24

Orion

I sat back watching Rizzo rubbed Tamia's hair. I still remember how Tamia told her that she faked sleep to get out of that house. I felt like I had let Rizzo down before I could build her up. In time, we finally spoke about Rizzo and Croy, and at first, the shit didn't bother me because she was with me now, and I knew she wasn't dealing with him anymore. But, knowing that my girl was with my brother fucked me up a little.

"Alright, we have everything she needs for discharge tomorrow. It has been fun, Ms. Tamia." The nurse smiled at Tamia, and she smiled back.

"So, why does she have to stay another day again?" Rizzo asked, looking down at her phone.

"Well, we ran a few labs, and we just want to get those back before we release her. Nothing too major." The nurse smiled and walked out of the room with the promise that she would bring Tamia more movies.

"I'm ready to go home, mommy. I don't like it here." Tamia cried, and Rizzo rocked her.

"We will. How about you take a nap and when you

wake up, it will be time to go?" Rizzo asked, and Tamia laid right on her chest and fell asleep. I watched Rizzo lay her down before she walked over and sat on my lap.

"I don't understand Orion. I know Croy was upset with me, but why take it out on Tamia?" Rizzo asked, rubbing her eyes.

Looking at her, you could tell she was tired, but Rizzo wouldn't rest until she knew Tamia was safe. Since the hospital didn't have proof that it was her father that did it, Croy could walk in and see Tamia if he wanted to. Rizzo didn't want to take the chance, but I did, it would be the end of Croy's career.

"I don't think my brother would hurt her, babe. I know you are looking at me like you want to kill me, but for real. Croy is dumb, but he loved his kids. That nigga wouldn't even beat Armon when he wrote all over his seats in his brand new cocaine white Range Rover," I said, and Rizzo laughed.

"I remember that. He came over pissed, and I had to run Armon to my mother's because Croy was scaring him with his yelling." Rizzo laugh quickly ended like she suddenly thought about something.

"I'm going to kill Tiffiah!" Rizzo jumped up, and I caught her before she reached the door. At the same time, someone knocked and entered. We both looked on and in walked Tamiko, peeking from the corner.

"Don't shoot, please," Tamiko joked, but Rizzo rushed to the door and gave her the biggest hug. I sat back and looked over Tamia to make sure she didn't wake.

"Babe, we are going to step outside and talk. Want something from the vending machine?" Rizzo asked, walking over to me and placing a kiss on my lips. The way she licked her lips afterwards made my dick rock up. Rizzo had been holding out, but I had been cooling with it. The only issue was my girl was a bad bitch, and everything she did made a nigga want to spread them legs and dive right in.

"Cool, stay close though. I got Tamia, and I need to make a call anyway." Rizzo kissed me again and leaned in. I grabbed her hand and placed it on my dick, making her smile.

"When I get back, we can find an empty room. I got you, baby." Rizzo pulled away, but Tamiko stopped her.

"I'm coming Riz, but I need to say something to Orion," Tamiko said, and Rizzo looked at her like she was crazy.

"Something like what?" Rizzo asked, turning around. I stood up and pulled her to me and kissed her neck.

"Tamiko, go ahead." I smiled and held Rizzo with my arms, both of us waiting to see what her friend had to say to me.

"I am sorry, Orion. I could have taken your friend out for my selfish ass reasons, and that wasn't right. I don't know you too well, but I can see you make my friend extremely happy. Don't fuck that up because I am an amazing shot if Truth hasn't already told you." Tamiko winked, and Rizzo laughed.

"My bitch!" Rizzo chanted.

"Shut up, but thank you, Tamiko. If you didn't know, Truth is good and awake. You should go and see him." I said, and Tamiko nodded.

"I don't know if he even wants to see me, and to be honest, I have come to terms that Truth and I are toxic to each other. I need to stay as far away from him as I can until I can resist his Asian charm." Tamiko laughed.

"Understood. You two go talk, we good." I walked over and hugged her. I watched them both walk out of the room as Tamia sat up.

"I thought they would never leave." She smiled, and I burst out laughing. I got up and went to sit beside her bed.

"Yo, you gotta chill with that fake sleeping shit. Your mom's crazy!" I laughed.

"Yeah, but she not here, and I can ask for stuff now." Tamia grinned and folded her arms.

"Who said I had some money? How do you know that I am not just a broke man out here, Tamia?" I asked, and she looked like she was thinking of what to say.

"I saw a receipt in your car with a lot of zeros. Step in my office, Uncle Orion," Tamia said, and I knew then that she had me wrapped around her little finger.

"Name your demands, but this is a one-time deal. Let mommy find out, and I am turning on you!" I pointed at her and made a silly face, and she tore up laughing.

Tamia told me everything she wanted when she got out of the hospital, and I was sending the list right over to one of my runners to pick up and deliver to the house. When Rizzo came back, she fussed us both out for Tamia still being awake and rocked her to sleep for real this time.

25

Rizzo

Once Tamia fell asleep, I pulled Orion out of the room to tell him what Tamiko said to me. When Tamiko stepped outside, I figured she had some heart-warming speech for me as well, but the bomb she dropped on me was a blessing for all of us.

"Lola tells me you haven't found Croy and Tiffiah yet," Tamiko said, leaning on the wall.

"Nope and Orion had been combing the streets for his ass. They just put a bounty out on his head, but no word yet." I shook my head. They couldn't have gotten too far. Both Croy and Tiffiah were about as smart as a bag of rocks.

"Check this, the other day I did laundry at the laundry unit at our building. I stepped out to go back home and sulk until the washer was done, but for some reason, I looked over at the Smiths," Tamiko said, and I was praying she didn't say what I thought she was going to say.

"There, I see Tiffiah, hauling groceries up to an apartment. The bitch wasn't even being sneaky about the shit and looked like she had an attitude. Girl, I sat back and watched her take trip after trip by *herself for the groceries. They are living in the Smiths, or at least laying low," Tamiko said, and I wanted to rush back in there and tell Orion everything.*

"So that nigga is laying right under our noses, we were asking around for Croy, and he is sending Tiffiah out. Did Tamiko give an apartment number?" Orion asked soon as I told him everything. Orion pulled his phone out and made a call.

"Yeah, 720B. You know I want answers before you take him to the airport, right?" I asked, and Orion looked at me like I was crazy.

"Airport?" he asked, and I winked my eye. Orion burst out laughing at my ass like I was the joke of the day.

"You know." I slit my throat to emphasize what I meant.

"Rizzo, all I want you to worry about is Tamia and our baby you are carrying now. How and when Croy gets dealt with will be on me. I got you both from here on out, okay," Orion said, and I backed away from his touch.

"Orion, this man let that bitch tear my baby's skin open. Even if Tamia is all smiled and giggles, they are saying that anything can trigger her memory and fuck her up for life. There is no way he moves from that fucking apartment and I not know about it." Orion pinched the bridge of his nose, and I knew I was pissing him off, but I was serious.

Beyond what Croy let happen to our child, Croy had hurt me time after time. There was nothing and no one who would tell me I wouldn't get him back for what he did to us. Orion was upset, and I get it, but it had nothing to do with my beef with Croy. Tamia was the final straw when it came to me.

"Rizzo, please don't try that urban book shit you read

about, okay? I am not them niggas, and you ain't them females. I need you to sit back and let me handle Croy, iight?" Orion asked.

I was going to agree, but he pissed me off. I just simply walked past him into the room with my daughter. Orion never joined me in the room, and I was okay with it for now. I watched Tamia sleep, and soon after, sleep took over myself as well.

———

"MOMMY, IS THIS OUR NEW HOUSE?" Tamia asked, looking out the window as Orion pulled up to the house.

"Yeah, maybe, baby girl," I said, and Orion gave me a look while he placed the car in park.

"Tamia, your Mimi is inside, how about you go in and see your room," Orion said.

"Is it how we discussed?" Tamia asked, and I whipped around looking at her. I had to stop talking around my daughter because she was becoming too much for me.

"Everything is specific." Orion winked, and I rolled my eyes at them with a sly grin. Tamia hauled ass into the house to see her room, while Orion looked at me but never said a word.

"Look, I would like to go inside and make my baby some dinner, so you want to talk or give me more orders?" I asked.

"Rizzo, I get that you don't like having to stay behind on this ride. I don't see my woman sneaking out to kill niggas while I'm at home looking stupid. If you handle him or Tiffiah, I want to be there to make sure they don't get the upper hand. Fair isn't good enough for me right now," Orion said calmly.

"I can defend myself Orion and—"

"MY CHILD CAN'T!" Orion yelled, and he wore this look that sent chills down my spine. "You think you can block every swing and hit? Rizzo, all I care about is you, and now you have given me Tamia and a new child to love as well. Let me do my job and protect you. If I need your help, I will reach out." Orion said, and I shook my head.

"Fine, but you better make the mother fucker suffer." I folded my arms, and Orion pulled me closer to him for a kiss.

"You owe me something too." He placed my hand on his dick, and I smiled. I forgot I offered Orion some pussy earlier.

"Fine, but in the back where we have tint." I jumped in the back, and Orion laughed at my ass. After telling me to be careful, Orion got out and came to the back, letting his seats down.

"I missed this wet pussy. I know that pussy gushy for daddy right now." Orion kissed my neck, talking nasty just how I liked.

Gently laying me down, Orion tried to fit his big frame between my legs. Instead, he had me in a half headstand while he devoured my pussy.

"Fuck! Eat that shit, daddy! Yessss, get nice and full off this pussy!" I moaned.

I loved the way Orion ate my pussy before he gave me some dick. Since everything happened, I have made him go without, and he was making good on his return to his pussy. I came soon after, and Orion pulled me on top of him.

"Ride this dick, bae." Orion slapped my ass, and I went crazy on Orion.

I didn't know if it was the hormones or what, but I lost

all control when Orion's dick reached my spot. Orion drove me crazy, and as upset as was with him, I loved him more and more each day. When this was all over, I planned to tell him just how much.

26

Truth

I was tearing my house up with the new Hoveround I was able to cop from this crackhead that owed me some money. Lola was having a fit and left my ass here, but I was good now that I had some wheels. The medication they gave me was putting me on my ass, so I ditched them when Lola left out for lunch earlier. I was waiting for Terrance to come through on something I had him looking into, and he should be pulling up soon. So, when the doorbell chimed, I assumed it was him.

"Hey." Tamiko waved and pushed her hands in her pockets. I just looked at shorty, and I could tell I was the reason she was looking worn out and stressed.

"Hey, uh, come on in." I rolled back, and Tamiko giggled a little as she walked in, looking around. "So, what's up, Killa?" I asked, and Tamiko looked down at her feet.

"I'm sorry, Truth. I know I fucked up shooting you and—"

Tamiko started, but I stopped her by pulling my gun out, aiming it at her.

"Yeah, but you didn't fuck up by shooting me. You fucked up by not killing me. What did I do so bad that you felt the need to dose me up with two holes?" I asked, and Tamiko looked down the barrel but didn't say shit.

"I... I don't know, Truth," she said, and I shook my head.

"I know I forced you to end my babies' lives, I know. Either way, Tamiko, I was owed more than that. We both fucked up, and I say we call it even," I said, putting my gun in my lap.

"What? So, we were even when I shot you. Why did you pull a fucking gun on me just now? You know what, don't even answer that, Truth. I only came here to tell you that I am done with us. We are toxic to each other. Each time I let you pull me in, it's me who ends up with the broken heart. I love you Truth, and I still do, but I must think of me for once. I mean, really think about me this time." Tamiko said, and she was pissing me off.

There was nothing toxic about us, but Tamiko had really made it seem that way.

"So, what now? You leave, and I never see you again?" I asked, being sarcastic. Tamiko rolled her eyes and shifted her weight.

"No, I still plan to be around, but I don't need you trying me in the meantime. If that's too much for you, I was offered a job in Georgia, and I have no problem taking it." Tamiko was serious, and I had never seen her in this form.

"Tight man, like I told you, I ain't for holding a female when she wants out. I love you too though Tamiko, and I must be honest with you, I ain't giving up on you. When the time is right, and I'm back on my feet, I plan to come for you and make shit right between us. We fucked up right now, but time might change things," I said, making Tamiko smile.

"Maybe, but for now, I just need you to respect my wishes and give me time to heal. I really am sorry, Truth, but I must go. My friend needs me, and I need to be there for her." Tamiko kissed me softly and walked to the front door.

"So, you did talk to Lola, huh?" I asked, turning and smiling back. Tamiko nodded before she opened the front door and walked to her car.

The hardest part was watching her walk out of my life. I know the pain that I caused Tamiko, and she made sure I would always remember. Tamiko had made a significant impact in my life, and from her sassy walk, I knew she would be good without me. It fucked me up to think about it, but maybe I was hurting Tamiko more and more with each day we went trying to make it work.

I shook the feeling off as I texted Lola and told her to come and get me. Terrance called a meeting ASAP. Lola planned to go to see Tamia, and I needed to catch the ride with Orion.

Once I was ready, Lola was already outside and ready to go. Since she hated to wait, I took my time just to fuck with her. I knew she wouldn't leave me helpless and crippled. Rolling into Orion's crib, I was confused when I saw Terrance standing there looking at Lola like she was a sirloin steak.

"Something wrong with your eyes, nigga?" I asked, and Terrance looked at me.

"This you, Truth? My bad," Terrance said and looked away.

"Boy, this is my brother, fuck him. Nice to see you again, Terrance." Lola said and walked to the backyard where Rizzo was.

"I got that thing you needed in my trunk," Terrance said and passed Orion the folder I had seen already.

I knew JB was suspect, but when I saw pictures of him supplying Croy, I knew it would piss Orion off and cut JB loose. I didn't like how he spoke to my sister anyway. What would really catch Orion's eye was the pictured of Rizzo cleaning up after JB and Croy had killed one of our own men.

"This nigga is working with Croy against us?" Orion asked, and Terrance nodded, giving him the full rundown.

"JB is in the trunk. With his hit list, he was about to send out on you and Truth, Croy sent him the payment. All of that is there in your hands though," Terrance said and motioned for us to follow him.

"Nah, take that nigga to the warehouse and end him there. I have a bigger fish to go and catch," Orion said.

Terrance gave the head nod before walking out the door. I made a mental note to see what was up between him and Lola when I was done with Orion.

"What you trying to do?" I asked, and Orion looked up from the papers at me.

"I bag 'em. You snag 'em." Orion was in rare form, but it was time we ended this war with Croy, way past time.

27

Croy

"Daddy, can I please go outside and play with the kids outside?" Armon begged me, and I was sick of his whining. I did two more lines and waved him off, nodding my head. I could hear his feet rushing out the door and the screen door slam. Tiffiah was supposed to be back soon, and I needed more drugs. This weak ass bullshit Orion was getting from JB was nothing compared to what I got. Tiffiah was on the way back from his crib with what I needed, and I would be sick without it.

I had my family shacked up in one of my ex shorty's crib. I made her keep her lease and keep it furnished, but she was only here when inspection came around. Tiffiah was sick of the shit, but after explaining it was either safe in here with me, or dead out there with my family, she jumped right on board.

"Armon, get the fuck in the house!" I heard her yell, and I was going crazy around her attitude. If my son weren't here, I would have been put a bullet in her head.

"What the fuck is wrong with you, and where is my shit?" asked, looking at an empty-handed Tiffiah.

"JB wasn't there, so I went to check on my daughter and momma. You got her out there living good, so why couldn't we?" she asked, and I shook my head.

"Because you dumb sour pussy having bitch, my brother is still getting work from JB. Weak ass work, but still business, so if they came by and saw Armon playing, how does that look, huh?" I asked, slapping her upside the head.

"Chill out, Croy. What's the difference here? He out there now." She said, and I covered my face with my hands. I heard footsteps running towards my door and knew it was Armon coming in like Tiffiah has asked.

"Daddy, look Uncle Orion here." Armon smiled and ran right back out the door. The look on my face made my brother smirk. Fear set in, and I knew I had to do something to get away.

"Don't think too long, bro. I got niggas surrounding this building, and it's best you come out quietly. Don't forget your bitch," Orion said just as we heard the back screen door slam. I got up and walked over to Orion, but the feeling of a blunt object going over my head stopped me and sent me to the floor. I looked to Orion looking over my body.

"All you had to do was protect her, and you failed her." Orion lifted his boots and knocked me out cold on the floor.

⊏━⊐

I WOKE up chained to a chair in a room with Tiffiah chained up the same way. Tiffiah was still out of it, but in front of me sat Rizzo with a look of revenge on her face. I could tell the baby was changing her already as her cheeks had plumped up and her hips were a little wider. Rizzo didn't know that I knew she was pregnant, but with it right in front of me it was clear as day, and I knew it was Orion's. Rizzo looked at me with so much hate and anger that I wish I had something to take the feeling away.

"Why?" she asked, and I shook my head. Tiffiah started to move, and Rizzo looked her way.

"This bitch," was all Tiffiah slurred as she woke up.

"Yeah, that bitch. You fucking tore my baby skin open because you couldn't touch me, huh?" Rizzo asked Tiffiah, and a slick grin crossed her face.

"I tore her little disrespectful ass up, yup! I sure did! I did what the fuck you were too afraid to do. Don't get mad at me. She was too weak to take it." Rizzo ended Tiffiah speech with two to the dome. I watched as Tiffiah's head went back with the first shot, and then the second went through the bottom of her chin and out the top of her head.

"Rizzo, I had nothing to do with it." I tried to plead to her, but Rizzo simply got up and walked out of the room.

I looked over at Tiffiah's body, and just then, Orion and my father walked in. I straightened up and tried to act hard for them. Here I was on my death bed, and I was still trying to fake it for the two people I looked up to.

"I see you two are here to finish me off. I mean, it's only right." I said, shaking my head. "Do the shit, Orion! You a man, do it!" I yelled as my father removed his gun and shot me four times in the chest and stomach.

The impact pushed me back, and it was getting harder to breathe. Blood filled my lungs as Orion walked over, towering me again.

"It was supposed to be us against the world. You chose this shit, bro. Sleep peacefully, brother." Orion pressed the cold steel against my temple and ended my life as I knew it.

28

One Year Later

RIZZO

"Mommy! Get Oni!" Tamia yelled from her room.

I smiled because Oni was finally crawling, and she was giving Tamia a taste of her own medicine. Orion ran upstairs in our brand new five-bedroom three-story house. Orion had kept his word and protected us as his family and placed a very gorgeous eighteen karat diamond ring on my finger as proof. After I gave birth to our daughter, Orion presented this house and two cars as the small gift. My baby went all Kanye West on my ass and bought a piece of Netflix and invested money in Amazon in my name. Orion also purchased the property of Harriston Homes and put the new units in my name, and I was good at overseeing the property. When I read all the paperwork and how much I owned, I felt like it was all a dream

"How long do we have to worry about those two?" Armon asked, and I shook my head.

"There's no telling, baby." I rubbed his head and pulled my famous baked Alfredo out of the oven.

We took Armon in due to us being his family. Orion had no issues getting him because he was biologically family, and of course, my baby's money was long. Since being with us, Armon had moved up a grade level, and no longer needed a tutor, but he asked to keep her. Orion swears his nephew had a crush on her, but I figured he liked the extra attention.

"Terrance, shut your ass up and bring Tamiko's roast out of the car!" Lola yelled, walking into the house.

Truth was right behind her, trying to get Tamiko to give him some.

"No damn, last time I fucked up and gave you some and tried to leave, you shot my fucking tires out. Bye Truth. Hey, girl." Tamiko hugged me, and Lola followed after putting her homemade yeast rolls in the kitchen.

"Girl chill, you were talking shit about this long dick!" Truth dapped up Terrance, but Lola gave Terrance a look, making me laugh.

"Lola, chill with your shit. You about to be bent over on that bench in Rizzo's bathroom in a few," Terrance said, and I looked at Lola, who was now trying to find everything and its momma to do, instead of looking my way.

"You been fucking in my bathroom, nasty ass?" I questioned, and Lola shook her head with widened eyes.

"Yeaaaahhhh, you have, little nasty," Tamiko said as she snuck a yeast roll.

"Shut up, preggo!" Lola yelled and covered her mouth. Tamiko looked like she wanted to curse Lola clean out, but I was about to beat her to it.

"Excuse me?" I asked, and Truth and Orion entered with Terrance right behind them.

"Who pregnant? Rizzo again, I bet." Truth laughed, and Lola and I just looked at Tamiko. "I know you lying, bae you pregnant?" Truth looked at Tamiko, and she rolled her eyes and walked out back with Truth and his questions on her heels.

"Damn, I thought I was about to have another one." Orion bent down and kissed me.

"I mean, I'm down if you with it. Let's go fifty on a little boy." I smirked, and Orion smacked me hard on the ass.

"Mommaaaaa, get Oni!" I moved away from Orion and went to see what Tamia was fussing about now. Sure enough, Oni was pulling her iPad charger out of the wall.

"Onika Lahey, why are you messing with your sister little mean butt. Tamia, you need to pick these play clothes up, and I mean now. Hurry up because dinner is almost done," I said, and Tamia locked her iPad before picking up her play dresses. I went back to see everyone else with Oni on my hip.

When I gave birth to Oni, it was easier than when I had Tamia. The best part was Orion never left my side. Marissa and my mother coached me so well, and I was blessed to have them both. Farrow and Farooq were out shopping for more shit than Oni needed, but she entered the world loved and as beautiful as the day itself. Orion still thanked me for being strong and helping him through. Once my water broke, the hard Orion was gone, and I had to coach him on what to do, but my baby was a trooper after that.

"Hey, daddy baby," Orion cooed, and I laughed.

It was still funny watching him in baby mode with Oni. Her chunky self was now Orion's complexion and looked just like him. Day by day, Tamia did too, and I was happy that I saw Orion when I looked at her and not Croy.

After everything happened with them, we found out that JB was fucking with him on everything. Lola was hurt, but Terrance swooped in and had been by her side the entire time. They just recently went public, and we all thought they were the cutest couple. Tamiko still holding out on being with Truth, but I know she had been fucking him. I was just waiting for proof, and now I had it. Looking at her, I could see the pregnancy glow looked so good on her.

"Damn, I hope my boy looks just like me too. Fuck it. Tamiko, you been with me through it all, and you carrying my baby confirms what I've been telling you. Stop fucking up the good vibes and marry a nigga." Truth said, getting on one knee.

"Get your ass up Truth, you sound stupid." Tamiko tried to get him off the ground, but he wouldn't move. Rolling her eyes, she looked up at all of us who were looking dead at her ass. "What?" she asked.

"You serious, ain't you, Tamiko?" I asked, and she rolled her eyes.

"Truth know damn well we are getting married one day, but not right now. I will not accept a pregnancy ring, fuck that. Thank you though, baby daddy." Tamiko bent down and kissed Truth, and he came to his feet.

"You cold, but I feel you. I'm just going to go and ask my other bitch." Truth turned, and Tamiko smacked him upside the head.

Looking around the room, I was happy. It was just that simple with us. My kids were out the hood and healthy, and my friends and I were in healthy and happy relationships. Gatherings like this had become a regular thing, and it felt good to have a family of my own. Momma Rose always told me I would have everything my heart desired when I let go. I was looking at the one thing I desired, and I had earned every piece of it. Kissing Orion, I continued to enjoy my family as we ate and discussed what's next for us all.

CPSIA information can be obtained
at www.ICGtesting.com
Printed in the USA
LVHW041704240120
644725LV00002B/380